THE WASP

It takes just one second to alter Kate Barlow's life. A wasp distracts her attention for just a second while she is driving one afternoon. But even this short time period is long enough to almost kill a child. From this terrifying experience stems her continually growing phobia against any buzzing insect . . . and a chilling series of events is set in motion.

ISBN 0 7540 8517 1

D1694754

THE WASP

Ursula Curtiss

First Published 1963
by
Dodd Mead & Co
This edition 1998 by Chivers Press
published by arrangement with
John Curtiss

ISBN 0 7540 8517 1

British Library Cataloguing in Publication Data available

Printed and bound in Great Britain by
Redwood Books, Trowbridge, Wiltshire

TO ELIZABETH WILMOT, *with love*

I

I<small>T TOOK</small> all of one second to alter Kate Barlow's fought-for life. What happened to her was undoubtedly duplicated in countless instances, that same day, all over the country. What happened after that—but there were no statistics available.

She was driving along a country road, and late-afternoon shadows slipped as coolly as water over the polished hood. With the hazards of traffic left behind, her hands were steady and almost easy on the wheel. On the back seat were groceries and a typed manuscript she had to deliver; beside her in the front seat, rambling on about the criminality of plumbers, sat her brother-in-law by marriage.

Perhaps because of that tenuous kinship, Kate had felt at ease with Gerald Symmes from the first, even when she still flinched from the others. He had not tried to cheer her up, and he had not reminded her astringently that she was not the first widow in the world or would she be the last. He had none of the strength of the Barlows; in the face of emergency he candidly folded up, and refreshingly, expected no more of other people.

Another shadow splashed by. ". . . a slimy track, like snails, from portal to portal," said Gerald musingly, and that was when Kate's world altered.

From somewhere on the floor of the car came a dry vicious buzz. Almost simultaneously a wasp flew up, stung furiously at the windshield, bounced there a moment and flew at Kate's face.

Some clear elastic portion of her brain had recognized the danger at once; in a way, like most drivers, she had always been prepared for it. Invading bees or wasps caused a certain number of highway accidents every year, and the newspaper accounts always seemed needlessly tragic. What was one sting, or ten, against a critical injury or even death? The driver simply had to brace himself and keep his attention grimly on the road until he found a safe place to pull up.

But all this did not take into account the violence of reaction. Kate swung her head blindly and the wheel followed; in the same flash of time the wasp buzzed angrily in the hair over her forehead and she gasped and stepped on the brake. The dappled emptiness of the road edge was swallowed under the wheels in gulps and jerks, and then— just before her brother-in-law's shout of horror? just after? —out of nowhere flashed a very small figure on a red tricycle.

The car rocked to a halt, but not before the right front wheel had felt the impact. Gerald made an indescribable sound, and Kate, heart beating in what felt like blinding strokes, got the door open and jumped out.

Somewhere in there was a stitch of time, which she tried to forget later, when she took in the total silence and emptiness of the road and realized that she had only to back, swerve, and be on her way. Being careful, of course, not to look and see what she had killed or maimed—

By that time she was around the front of the car, staring at a small blond boy who was struggling to his feet on the dusty road edge. Cheek and arm and leg were beginning to redden under the rough stripes of dirt, but he wasn't dead. Kate sent up a prayer about that, because even her corner-of-the-eye glimpse of the tricycle, a crumple of red under her near wheel, made her stomach turn over. He had jumped off it, or been flung free. . . .

She said in a spent voice. "I'm awfully sorry. Are you hurt?" and the words seem to rattle about under the trees. Surely windows would be flung up now, indignant mothers converge, fathers arrive to threaten—but nothing happened at all. The boy, who might have been four years old, stared back at her out of round, brightened blue eyes. Kate wished that he would cry, or run, or rub the places that must be stinging like fire, but he simply stood there. She took a careful step forward, stretching her hand out and down, and said, "I'm sorry about your tricycle, I'll get you a new one. Can we go in now and see your mother?"

The boy's hands disappeared instantly behind his back, but he began to trudge toward the opening in the green hedge. A small picket gate was open; that, of course, was what he had shot through, down the tilting cement walk. He could so easily be lying broken and still under her wheel . . . Kate's legs began to shake with reaction. To control herself she fixed her attention so desperately on this particular patch of the world that she seemed absorbed into it, as much a part of the scene as the daisies in the uncut grass, and Gerald's call was bewildering.

Turning, she saw his face at the car window as though it were a stranger's: long, pale, rather like a courteous and well-read goat's. He called, "I'll come in with you," and Kate shook her head violently. Gerald, badly frightened, would bluster—and in front of her, up two cement steps, the little boy had opened the door of the house.

Later, she remembered the room in detail, and the man's face; at the moment there was only the shocked "Barney!", the furious glance that raked her before he dropped to his heels and began examining the child. Kate said tightly,

"I can't tell you how sorry—I don't think I actually hit him, I was—" and she might not have been in the room at all.

"Hurt here, Barney?" The man was flexing the thin scratched arm, probing the T-shirted shoulder. "Here?"

The round blond head shook. Kate realized with a spreading coldness that the child hadn't made a sound since picking himself up out of the dirt—but that was fright, surely, and nothing to do with the dully shining graze on his temple?

Yes, because the man tilted the averted face to his, said, "Okay, Barney?" and, at the boy's silent nod, stood up again. The tension had gone out of the room, but Kate's shoulders still ached and the hand with which she extended her driver's license shook a little.

He read it and handed it back; he said in a neutral voice, "What happened?"

Kate told him, deliberately including the wasp. She knew with despair that it was happening all over again, the thing she had thought she was cured of: first came the sudden dampness of her skin, then a feeling that she was not standing on a level surface, then the final frightening conviction that if she moved the focus of her glance, it would be the room that moved instead.

She said carefully, "Could I—?" and dropped down on the edge of a flowered chair. It was surprisingly hard and unwelcoming. "I didn't see your little boy at all until it was too late, he just—appeared. Whatever you want to do about a doctor . . . and if you have a telephone I have to report this to the police, don't I?"

"Barney," said the man abruptly without taking his eyes from hers, "go get cleaned up before your mother sees you."

The boy disappeared at once; he had, Kate realized, left no imprint on the room at all, but then it was not a room that would take kindly to imprints. It was a painfully clean and polished Parlor, furnished with what was called

10

a suite, a beady-eyed parakeet in an ornamental cage, a vase of artificial flowers, and then left sternly alone.

"Look," said the man sensibly to Kate, "my wife's sick." He nodded at the inner regions of the house. "Nervous breakdown, I guess you'd call it—her father died last week and she's all to pieces about it, cries all day, won't eat, won't let the kid out of her sight except when she's asleep. If we got the police in here, and she found out Barney'd been in the road—"

Water ran somewhere: Barney at his ablutions. Kate supposed that with his mother ill he had had to learn a certain amount of self-sufficiency; nevertheless she winced at the thought of all those dirt-ingrained scrapes. The rush of sound had evidently waked the woman, because a drowsy voice with an edge to it began to call from somewhere, "Mitch? . . . Mitch?"

The man's face was instantly transformed with worry. "There. See?" He bundled Kate rapidly to the door. "Yes, all right, if there's anything wrong I'll call you—"

It was deliverance, thrust upon her. Kate clung to that all the way to the car.

Gerald, who had the perception of another female at times of crisis, produced a cigarette and match in silence before he said comfortingly, "Wasn't *that* ghastly. Tricycles ought to come under the Sullivan law. Are you all right?"

"Reasonably." The sick dizziness had passed; in its place was an impulse to talk shakily and too much. Kate said with great calm, "I'm just—I have to sit here a minute."

"Take your time," said Gerald, and gave one of his disarmingly helpless laughs. "On another occasion let's bring a drink. I killed the wasp, by the way."

Kate half-finished her cigarette, wanting to linger with it, knowing she must not. The crushed tricycle had to be backed away from, and she turned the key in the ignition, put the car in reverse, released the brake, glanced into the rear-view mirror, and switched off the engine. She said simply, "Will you drive? I can't."

11

Georgia Barlow, her mother-in-law, would have been patient and ruthless, forcing her to overcome this new terror; Joanna Symmes, her sister-in-law and Gerald's wife, would have taken the wheel with a kind of angry contempt. It was the old principle of getting back on the horse that had thrown you (although why, Kate had always wondered? Why not just take up some other sport?) but sometimes, like a number of laudable things, it was wearing.

Gerald, not himself a getter-back-on-horses, said merely, "Sure," and they changed places. Kate lit another cigarette, put it out, and stared silently through the windshield. "Mitch" was evidently a nickname; the mailbox had said J. Maynard. . . .

Presently, rounding a curve, Gerald said, "You did *not* lose control of the car, if that's what you're thinking."

"Oh, yes, I did. When the wasp—"

"It wouldn't have made any difference. When someone runs directly in front of your car without warning, you're not responsible. I was a witness, I'll tell the police—"

Kate explained about the police. She felt surprisingly defensive, even with Gerald, but he only shrugged. "Oh, well, all the better. The child certainly seemed all right. I'm not even sure you touched him."

Had she? Had the impact under her right front wheel been tricycle or child? Kate closed her eyes, trying to synchronize sight and sensation, and as though she had invited it into her brain something gave a sudden dry buzz directly behind her.

She did not make a sound, but Gerald checked the car at her involuntary motion forward on the seat. After an over the shoulder glance he said mildly. "It's only a leaf."

"Sorry." How wasp-like and vicious it had sounded, that innocent leaf . . . Kate's own backward glance had shown her the manuscript in its box, ready to be delivered to Mr. Carpenter—who was not, however, expecting it until tomorrow. She would just as soon not face him at the

12

moment; he was much too observant at the best of times. The typing therapy had been her own idea as much as Georgia's, but she always felt, in Carpenter's presence, like an insect about whom a monograph was being written.

Gerald had evidently looked at the boxed manuscript without seeing it, or possibly he only wanted to get home and into a chair and have a drink. Home . . . well, not quite that, for Kate—or perhaps it was more, a refuge that held her own safe inviolable corner. Unless they were in danger of losing them, people seldom clung to their normal everyday homes as she had clung to this place.

There it was, around a curve, long and chimneyed under sheltering elms. Oyster-white shutters softened the severity of its charcoal clapboards, and brass shone on the knockers of its two red-chalk front doors. One of the doors, almost swallowed in lilacs, was Kate's.

Gerald swung the car into the shadowed drive, stopped it, and let out a heartfelt sigh. "Made it," he said, and then, in an odd awkward tone, "Kate, you know something? If I were you I wouldn't mention . . ."

His olive eyes were somber under their drooping lids, but that was an accident of nature; Gerald could look brooding over the selection of a sandwich. Still, it might have been instinct that lifted Kate's hand to her forehead in a half-forgotten gesture, curving a scallop of pale caramel hair closer over the scars it hid. She said, "What wouldn't you mention?" and Gerald said, "Oh—nothing. Coming . . . ?"

He went off, grocery-laden, to the main part of the house, and Kate walked across the grass to her own door. The late sunlight was warm and still, and a wasp walked delicately across the screen, wings lifted over its segmented brown body. For an absurd moment Kate thought it had come with her from the car, this near-agent of destruction.

She had never been fond of wasps— certainly real devotees must form a very small part of the population, or consist of other wasps, but this morning she would have stood warily back as far as she could reach and opened the screen door to dislodge it. Now, with the memory of the dry rush at her face, the furious buzzing in her hair, she walked rapidly away, and when she came back a few moments later the wasp was gone.

Such a simple, instinctive thing. Six steps across springy, leaf-patterned law, six steps back. The first rung in the ladder to destruction.

II

THE apartment—small sitting room, bedroom and bath—
was wonderfully cool and quiet. Originally an unused barn,
it had been remodelled by Mr. Symmes at the time of
his son's marriage to Joanna Barlow. Joanna, however, had
preferred to live in the main house, particularly when it
was pointed out by Georgia that, Mr. Symmes, having sum-
marily withdrawn from the scene, the apartment would
be a financial burden unless it were rented. Kate's occupancy had privided a solution welcome to everybody although it had to be kept secret from Mr. Symmes, who
in his present unrecalcitrant mood was quite capable of un-
remodelling it again, down to the last wisp of hay and
nest of mice.

Kate showered and dressed and, in order not to stop
moving, went into the little sitting room, whose lowset
windows were like summer landscapes hung vividly on its
pale gray walls, and tidied sheets of carbon and manuscript beside her typewriter. There was no one to see all
this brisk activity; it was a statement to herself that she
was perfectly all right. Horrified at herself for having lost
control of the car, and badly shaken at a near-fatality, but
still all right. The thing to remember was that it had not
been a fatality; the thing to forget was the brief terrifying
blur through her windshield.

But the blur had been trees this time, and not cruel red
rock. And, ten months ago, it had been Robert who was
driving . . .

. . . and saying, to Kate's suggestion that she take the wheel for a while, "All right, when I find a place to pull off. This road must have been laid out with a corkscrew."

It was not narrow, but steep and winding, poised at times over a vast landscape that looked to Kate like something heaved up from a caldron. She had been Mrs. Robert Barlow for a month, and the business trip to Arizona was like an extension of their Canadian honeymoon.

New brides did not usually say anything forceful under the circumstances, and when the road began to straighten a little she only put out her cigarette and, with an air of imminence, undid her seat belt. Robert was not wearing his; they had been on horseback the day before, both for the first time in years, and he kept shifting position and observing wryly that there must be somewhere else to sit on.

Still, Kate was not really worried, although it was now almost four o'clock and he had been driving since eight that morning, with only a stop for lunch and a further leg-stretching pause for coffee. Robert was a safe and skillful driver; from time to time, as the afternoon light changed and violet began to lap coolly into the ruddy distances he would say, "Look over there, Kate," but his own glance away from the road was the merest flicker.

How long before the curve? When Kate dreamed about it it was a great india-rubber thing, beckoning them as though it had sat there for centuries, waiting for just this car and this second in time. In actuality it was a crescent of road around a chimney of red rock.

The car continued the crescent. There was no time for anything, not even a scream.

Kate woke to a world which had been moved a short distance away so as not to bother her. Nurses spoke softly but imperatively to her: she must take this pill, and this, and she must not touch the gauze over her forehead. The lower part of her back was an agony, even when she was moved with the utmost delicacy to a hard table; she thought drowsily, "We stayed too long on those horses," and then she remembered the car and knew that they had crashed.

Robert was obviously hurt worse than she; otherwise, even in the hospital, he would have managed to send word to her. Kate asked the nurses, several times, but perhaps her voice did not come out as she thought it did because they only said smilingly, "You're much better today, aren't you, Mrs. Barlow?" or "May I brush your hair for you? Such a lovely color, and you'll feel much cooler . . ."

She had been in the hospital four days before she learned that Robert was dead, killed instantly when the car crashed.

Kate ought to have guessed, from the brightly-masked look of Georgia's stony face, but she did not, and she went tremblingly to pieces. No one seemed to understand that it was horror as well as grief. In waking moments, less drugged than usual, she had thought, "Robert has a brain injury, and they won't tell me yet," and had gone on to make her own hazy, wary plans. Brain specialists . . . but she would nurse him herself; he would respond to her far sooner than to a stranger in a white uniform . . .

And all the time, through the wakings and wonderings how he was and what they would say to each other from their wheel chairs when his finally came through the door, he had been dead and bundled away forever.

If they had not told her that, what else had they not told her? They assured her that she would walk again, but was that merely a piece of bland comfort to tide her over another day?

Kate's temperature went up that night, and it was two days before she was allowed to see her mother-in-law again. They were both so artificially controlled, she thought later, that Robert might have been a broken tea-cup. Georgia said brightly that Kate was looking much better, and Kate thanked her for the bottle of imported sherry she had sent the day before. "Well, flowers are nice," said Georgia apologetically, "but you can't drink them."

Only at the end of her visit did Georgia crack. She was standing before the mirror over the bureau, putting up an automatic hand to the expertly honeyed hair she wore piled high and twisted. At fifty-odd, Kate thought randomly, she was a remarkably pretty woman, tall and firm-figured, with a soft heart-shaped face so devotedly creamed and lotioned that only along her throat and under her blue eyes was the skin even faintly crumpled. Even her voice and her easy idle laugh were soft, something under velvet—and then suddenly all the softness and prettiness fell away, and the mirrored face was as bleak and cold as stone.

"I suppose they've told you that crying helps," said Georgia harshly to Kate's reflection. "Well, it doesn't. If you cry it leaves you one last thing to do, if you absolutely have to."

That did not happen again. Under Georgia's lushness was the purest steel, and a great deal of practicality. She had been brought up in a Colorado mining camp, and she met with a head-on calm situations which most other women could not have borne without artificial props. Only once did she refer directly to the crash. She said that the car had evidently struck the rock chimney with an impact that sent it hurtling back across the road, turning over and throwing Kate and Robert clear in the process. Although the car was badly smashed up, the authorities had been able to determine that there had been no mechanical failure.

"I knew he was tired," said Kate, gazing steadily at her hands, "but we'd been talking just a minute before and the curve wasn't—"

A nurse arrived with a thermometer then, and she realized in the little silence the contradictory thing she had been about to say, because obviously the curve had been that bad. A driver didn't necessarily have to go to sleep at the wheel; all it took was a second of inattention, a late reflex. . . .

Little by little, it came to be assumed by both women that Kate would go back East with Georgia and stay with the Barlows, at least temporarily. For one thing, there would be papers to sign; Kate knew that she was executor of Robert's will, but beyond that she had no idea of where she stood financially. It was not a subject that came up in a month of marriage.

For another, there was the disturbing thing that attacked her as soon as she was allowed to walk up and down the halls. It usually came about as a result of sudden motion near her—a nurse turning quickly around a corner, or an elevator door whisking open—and instantly her palms were wet and she had a sensation of lurching. The doctor assured her that it was nerves and that she would not fall, but Kate came to dread her daily walks.

The deciding factor was Georgia's frank appeal, because in spite of her soft voice and her limpid gaze Georgia could be almost dismayingly frank. "Kate dear, if paying for the apartment would make you feel better, I won't exactly throw up my hands in horror. That old monkey Symmes, Joanna's charming father-in-law, pays Gerald an office boy's salary, which makes things a little . . . And not only that," said Georgia, lowering her voice and widening her eyes significantly, *"he is thinking of marrying again."*

This was obviously a matter of the utmost seriousness. Kate knew nothing of her mother-in-law's financial affairs; she did know—from Robert, dryly—that old Mr. Symmes, at eighty-odd, was expected to exit gracefully and soon, leaving the Symmes hardware money to fall like a plum into the hands of his only son. It was bad enough that he had taken a stern view of Gerald, expecting him to work; if he should marry again . . .

Unexpectedly and for the first time in weeks, Kate laughed. She said, "Oh, you can't have that," and Georgia said soberly, "Of course not, but he's terribly difficult . . ."

Kate left the hospital seven weeks after she had entered it, eight pounds thinner and rackingly unsure of herself; even the taxi ride to Georgia's motel was a braced, edge-of-the-seat affair. The shaved hair over her temple had grown, but wispily, and she felt that the purple scars shouted through it. Her eyes, a cool surprising gray instead of the brown they ought to have been, were so haggard that they gave her the look of an overworked actress.

She put herself docilely into Georgia's hands, then and when they reached the house in Connecticut. Georgia was everything she was not, bland, outgoing, comfortably interested in the details of everything, and Kate knew instinctively that it was good for her. Nightmare fell to the wayside before the relative merits of Vichyssoise as opposed to creamed asparagus for lunch. Gerald was as easy to be with as a cloud, and Joanna's crisp matter-of-factness was a help in spite of her haunting physical resemblance to Robert.

Little by little, by means of long rides through the spring-starred countryside, they got Kate used to the front seat of a car again. Resuming her driving was something else. That was an irrational fear, because she had not been at the wheel in Arizona, but still it was there, and she practiced as shakily as a beginner in the driveway and then on quiet back roads before she dared go anywhere near traffic.

Gradually she lost her haggard look, and one day when Joanna said reflectively, "You know, your hair is really stunning like that," she was startled; she had forgotten that the scars were there. The sudden flashes of instability, the helpless feeling of standing in a tilted world that might dissolve at any moment, vanished almost without her realizing it.

Until today. But that was only natural, thought Kate, locking her fingers tightly; it was not every day that one nearly killed a little boy. How terrifiedly silent he had been, even to his father's frantic questions . . . Could she have swerved the car, or might she have seen the child sooner if it had not been for the rattling and buzzing in her hair?

20

But he was not seriously injured, he could not be, or they would have had a doctor by now and called her.

Someone knocked loudly and peremptorily on the apartment door.

III

"DID I startle you? Sorry," said Joanna Symmes a moment later. "I knocked before, but then I thought you might be in dressing . . . Come and have a cocktail."

With her back to the melted-gold end of the day, she looked more than ever like a fencer, lean and springy and so precise that it was impossible to imagine an extra inch or ounce anywhere. Robert had had the same quality of sureness, but in his older sister it went further: here, even at a glance, was one of those magical beings who had known in the cradle exactly how much to tip, what invitations it was safe to accept, and whether a dress had really been reduced from two hundred dollars.

Just behind her head, with its short cap of dark curls, something flew in a lazy arc. Kate said involuntarily, "Close the door, will you?" and Joanna gave her a startled look and stepped inside, letting the screen door fall to. "Gerald told us about this afternoon. I hope you haven't been sitting here brooding."

Brooding about Robert, did she mean or about the little boy who had so narrowly escaped death? But then the very act of brooding would be distasteful to Joanna; she was far too definite and impatient a person for such mental untidiness. Whatever she had done was done, possibly not for the best, but irrevocably. It must, Kate thought suddenly, be a very comfortable way to live.

She smiled carefully at Joanna, to show that a single incident was not going to reduce her to the shaken creature over whom they had all worked so long and patiently. "Not exactly," she said, "but I would love a cocktail."

Because in the beginning it had been a necessity, Kate had fallen into the habit of having most of her meals at the house. There was nothing ceremonious about any of them. Georgia rose at an implacable six o'clock, winter and summer, so there was coffee at any hour after that; hungrier, non-dieting souls could forage for anything else. As lunch was equally haphazard, it was only at dinner that they were usually all together.

Tonight, for the first time in weeks, Kate was conscious of solicitude. Perhaps to make her feel at ease, Georgia launched into a detailed accounts of cats and dogs who had dashed fatally under her wheels, and, once, a horse. "It came out of nowhere, the size of a house—I suppose it was bolting—and before I knew it there it was, draped over the hood. They had to call a policeman to shoot it, and it was really a shame, such a beautiful animal. . ."

Kate poked blindly at her salad. Gerald said soberly to himself, "The life you save may be a horse's," and drew a sharp glance from Georgia.

"The point is," said Joanna in her crispest voice, "that these people—Maynard?—couldn't possibly hold you responsible in any case, Kate. The fact that you were able to stop when you did proves you weren't speeding. If there's any blame anywhere it's in letting a child that age have a tricycle so near the road."

All of it true . . . wasn't it? Except that if Kate had faced the wasp stoically her vision would not have been distracted; she would probably have been able to veer away from the tricycle.

"What matters is not making a mountain of it," said Georgia practically. "You did drive on home, didn't you, Kate?"

Here came the inevitable and possibly justified censure. Kate opened her mouth, and Gerald, who usually ate with an aloof and preoccupied air, like a butler forced to sit down with the family, lifted his head surprisingly. "Certainly she did," he said. "*I* think it took nerve."

After a second's astonishment, Kate let the lie stand. Like most lies it was much easier than the truth, and to contradict it might turn out to be a very wearying affair. Joanna was as ruthless as an hourglass, and Georgia would quote chapter and verse from one of the best-sellers about conquering fear, or self-discipline, or some other strong-minded theme. (Kate sometimes thought wistfully about a book encouraging cowards. "If you are afraid of large dogs, avoid those friends who keep them. If you have a terror of heights, stay away from them; simply explain that you have never cared for views . . .")

"Anyway, you're insured," said Joanna briskly, and then to Gerald, with the air of departing a subject permanently, "Did you know that your father took Mrs. Holden to lunch again today?"

Gerald raised a face of alarm. "He didn't."

"Oh, but he did," said Joanna grimly. "*And* they had two brandies afterward and he bought her flowers on the way out. Nan Mills told me. That's the third lunch this week."

"It's really shocking," said Georgia indignantly. "She can't be more than forty-five. When you think of a man your father's age, it's most unsuitable."

Gerald gave a little gloomy laugh. "Not to speak of all that money," he said baldly. "Well now, let's see, what can we . . ."

Usually, Kate listened with a mild amusement to the unflagging campaign to keep Gerald's father from remarrying; it had so far included an anonymous letter and a handkerchief drenched in rose geranium, a scent which made old Mr. Symmes violently ill and angry. She held no particular brief for the Barlow interest, but neither did she for Mr. Symmes, who after indulging Gerald in idleness for forty-odd years, as the heir to the Symmes hardware money, had suddenly turned upon him as a ne'er-do-well.

Tonight she let the talk wash over her head; little by

little, another room became realer than this one. A small painfully stiff room, with cheap hard furniture and a vase of artificial flowers instead of a great bowl of roses. A woman's voice called into it, drowsy and fretful, unaware of the crushed tricycle and the little boy washing away blood and dirt all by himself . . . ("Anyway, you're insured," said Joanna's crisp dismissing voice.)

Another voice said, "Kate's asleep."

"I am not," said Kate, and sat straighter, pushing her hair back. "Let's get some of these things out of the way . . ."

When she went back to the apartment, there was a wasp in her bathroom.

Wasp, or hornet? It was big, a dark, cold brown, with the suspended part Kate though of as landing gear. It had been crawling up the window frame in the dim glow of the mirror light she had left burning; at the sudden stir when the door was pushed wider it flew. With a little shock of fear Kate snatched the door shut and stood there gripping the knob ridiculously.

This would have to stop; she knew it quite clearly. Although she had grown up in Philadelphia, meeting Robert quite by accident at a houseparty there, there had been the usual intervals at camp, and wasps and bees were an integral part of climbing trees and sleeping in tents and all the other summer occupations of children. She had been stung often; she could remember being plastered with moist bicarbonate of soda, or, if she were at a distance from the camp, mud. Up to a certain age she had roared with pain and surprise; after that an occasional white-centered swelling was a matter of nonchalance and pride.

But it has always been the actual sting she minded, never the wasp itself, the delicate venomous organism that could conceal itself in the lining of a sleeve, the fold of a towel, the crevice of a car seat—

Kate stopped herself there. Moving very quickly, she

got her broom from its closet, advanced on the bathroom door, flung it wide.

Nothing buzzed or crawled anywhere. The window shone blankly back at her, the towels were innocent on their racks, the pale blue tile was unflawed. But it was here somewhere, it had to be. It took all her courage to twitch the shower curtain violently; the plastic folds only settled back whisperily on themselves.

Above and behind her came a mocking dry rattle of wings. Kate whirled, saw the wasp hovering over the lintel, and aimed wildly with the broom.

If she had killed it then—

But she did not. It soared away from her, buzzed briefly in the bedroom, floated on into the sitting room, making an angry stab at the ceiling from time to time, and settled down to a lively crawl on the striped couch. Kate watched it from the doorway, heart pounding foolishly; once again she had the feeling that this wasp knew her, and was only waiting for her to come closer before it attacked.

"Kate?" called a voice from the darkened lawn. "You left your cigarettes, and I didn't know whether you had any more . . ."

It was Georgia, and deliverance. Told that Kate was hunting a wasp, her mother-in-law said, "Where?" and picked up a magazine and killed it with two deft swats. "What a nasty looking thing," she said in her easy voice, and exhibited the corpse for Kate's inspection. "I killed one like it in my room this morning—there must be a nest somewhere. I'll get Gerald to look tomorrow, I hate the things."

Kate made what was meant to be a clinical inspection of the dead wasp, and it looked vicious and purposeful even now. Georgia dropped it into an ashtray. "Did you get stung this afternoon?"

Kate said no, that the wasp had apparently been too entangled in her hair to know what it was about, and Georgia said curiously, "Oh, I thought—" and let that die away. Almost apologetically, she handed Kate a red and white capsule. "You probably won't need this, but I know you finished your sleeping stuff weeks ago so I brought you one of mine. Just in case you wake up in the night and feel sort of jittery."

She had a faintly guilty air, as though she had slipped past Joanna with the sleeping capsule; in ways, Kate thought, Georgia seemed younger than her daughter. She said genuinely, "Thanks, I'll feel better just knowing it's there."

Georgia was easily demonstrative by nature; she leaned forward now and kissed Kate's cheek. "Get a good sleep, and don't worry about anything," she said.

When she had gone, Kate emptied the wasp out of the ashtray, read inattentively for a while, gave it up, and got ready for bed. She only discovered by accident, looking for a cleaner's ticket in her wallet, that as far as the little Maynard boy went she was not insured at all. Her driver's license had lapsed five weeks ago.

In the morning, without saying anything to anybody, Kate mailed a note and a check including a voluntary fine to the Bureau of Motor Vehicles and hoped for the best. She was horrified at the number of policemen she had passed in the last five weeks; she shrank equally from the recriminations which would pour down on her head for such carelessness—and quite rightly. Even Gerald would be appalled. They would all say, "But you must have gotten the notice," and undoubtedly she had, and put it aside because it always came in advance and she was doing something else at the time.

Who would believe, now, that Maynard had asked her not to report the accident?

Kate was having a second and solitary cup of coffee in Georgia's immaculate kitchen when the extension there rang. Joanna had left to drive Gerald to his despised job at the Symmes plant; Georgia, Kate knew, spent this period of the morning at a surprisingly businesslike desk in her room, checking to a penny the Barlow resources and indebtedness. When the phone rang twice more she picked up the receiver, and a man's voice said, "Sorry to bother you so early, Georgia, but is Kate around?"

It was Carpenter. Kate straightened militantly in the empty kitchen, thinking what a mistake this whole project had been on her part, and said, "This is Kate. If you were worried about your manuscript—"

"Not at all," said Carpenter's voice with the sunniness of bad temper. "I wondered if you had thrown it away or something. It's very dull at just about this point, I know."

"—it's in the car," said Kate as though she had not been interrupted. "I'm sorry, I thought you didn't want it until this afternoon. I'll—"

—what? Explain everything to Georgia, with all that entailed? Or force herself to drive again, sticking carefully to the back roads? One day could hardly matter after five weeks; the day that mattered was gone, irretrievably.

Carpenter said more temperately, "I'd come and get it myself but I've got a flat. I don't suppose you fix flats?"

"I'm afraid not." She had been light with Carpenter once; she would not be, soon again. "Would half an hour be all right?"

"Half an hour would be fine."

Kate went back to the apartment and changed her dress. She always dressed consciously for Carpenter now; had ever since the evening then, seated across from her in a restaurant, he had said dryly, "Don't worry, Kate, your virtue is safe with me. I will respect your—" he had carefully not glanced at the ice-gray pleats she wore on that hot night "—weeds."

She still got angry thinking about it, mostly at herself for the foolish assumption that it was possible to carry on any kind of relationship with a man without a misunderstanding arising somewhere. She had not demurred when Georgia and Joanna said firmly that it was time she started meeting people again, and when Carpenter had been casting about for a typist she had welcomed the work. Her typing was fast and accurate, and although it was not a nine-to-five job, it was a step toward one.

How had it changed, along the way? The first dinner invitation: Kate suspected that Georgia had arranged that, because they were all going to a pre-wedding party and it seemed wiser that Kate should be busy that evening. Carpenter was an intelligent and amusing companion, and she had found a surprising pleasure in simply being out of the apartment. It had not occurred to her until too late that he might think she was bored with being a widow.

The grimmest dress she owned was brown linen; it had looked, even when she bought it, like something for a wardress on her day off. Kate put it on, adjusted herself for Carpenter's critical eye, and was on her way to the door when the telephone rang.

Georgia would answer it in the house; this extension would only ring again if the call were for Kate. She watched it, fingers waiting on the doorknob, and after a moment or two it rang again.

"Mrs. Barlow?" She knew his voice at once, even before he said, "This is Mr. Maynard—Barney's father. You said to call you if anything . . . Well, the doctor's on his way, and I thought you might maybe want to be here."

She had known; she had known all night. "Yes," said Kate shakenly to the opposite wall. "Yes, I'll—I'll be right over."

IV

THE drive to Maple Avenue was a nightmare of dogs, stop signs and wandering children. What should have been a ten-minute run took Kate close to half an hour. She had rolled the car windows up against wasps, and she drove like a snail in the hot, airless interior. It seemed to her a marvel that she had ever had the windows open on these still sunny days, inviting wasps and bees and anything that flew.

But then the world looked entirely different now, embroidered with sharp hovering shadows, every one of them venom-laden. Bicycles seemed to rush suicidally at her, children chased balls expertly close to the road. The engine faltered, quickened cautiously, faltered again. Policemen looked for just such drivers, obviously rattled and unsure of themselves . . . Kate drove damply, grimly on.

And here was the house, and there was no avoiding it; it was like school to be gone to, only much worse. Although the doctor had not come yet—there was only a black Chevrolet, iridescent with age, in the driveway—the place had an air of silent crisis. Three quarts of milk sat on the sunny doorstep, nothing stirred at any of the windows.

She got out of the car, feeling eyed and hated from behind the blind panes, trying to stiffen herself. How distant Joanna's crispness seemed now, how hollow Georgia's comfortable assurance that she had not been to blame. This was an entirely different world, and she felt it engulf her again as she walked up the path between the squares of rough grass.

Even without the red-rimmed eyes and general look of distraction, the woman who opened the door was obviously Mrs. Maynard. Illness and worry had pinched and sharpened what might have been a delicate face, and she clutched at her robe with an air of habit, as though she lived in it. Pale blue eyes stared at Kate less with hostility than a kind of wonder, much as a motorist who had had a puncture might regard the nail that had done the damage.

She said, "I suppose you're the—you're Mrs. Barlow."

It was not quite an accusation, but Kate's head came up very slightly. "Yes—how is your little boy?"

"We're waiting for the doctor now. I don't know where he can be," said Mrs. Maynard. She sounded tired and querulous, as though she had been saying this for some time. Her gaze went peeringly to the road and came back to Kate's face. She said abruptly, "Do you want to come up and see Barney? He just might talk for you."

Oh, God. The thing Kate had feared. Silently, because there seemed nothing to say, she followed the angular flowered back up uncarpeted stairs and around a short turn of hall to an open doorway. Through it Maynard's voice was reading awkwardly, "But the giraffe was still sad because his tie kept slipping down, so he—"

Mrs. Maynard said too brightly, "Here's a lady to see you, Barney," and Kate, heart thumping, stepped into the small blue-walled room. It smelt faintly pine-scented, perhaps something to do with the parakeet, whose cage had been removed from the living room and now stood in a corner. Barney had been staring at the little bird while his father read; at Kate's approach he turned his head.

"Hello, Barney." She must not look appalled at the pallor of the small face, marked with rust-colored scrapes and an ugly blue bruise at the temple; most of all, she must not appear to notice the unnatural wideness and steadiness of the round gaze. Pretend it was a bad cold, something you

31

commiserated with, but lightly. "I came to see you about your tricycle."

There was a flicker of something—fright?—in the child's expression. Kate went on, committed but crushingly sure that whatever she said would turn out to be the wrong thing, "I owe you a new one, but it's been a long time since I had a tricycle and I don't know what kind to get."

Had there ever been such silence?

"You must know what kind you'd like," said Kate desperately, and was aware that behind her the Maynards were holding their breath and concentrating, too. Mrs. Maynard's perfume warred delicately with the pine.

Barney's throat tensed, his lips moved fractionally. The effort stopped so suddenly that it might have been a wishful illusion. Mrs. Maynard turned out of the doorway with a sigh that sounded like a sob, and her husband said in a pleading voice, "Alice, it'll be all right . . . Alice—"

In the driveway, tires crunched, a car door slammed. Kate, who was nearest the window, looked out and down at a green car hood, an M.D. clamped to the license plate, a purposeful man with a black bag hurrying up the walk. She said with relief, "Here's the doctor."

The doctor, whose name was Henderson or Sanderson or Pendleton—Mrs. Maynard all but swallowed it in her eagerness—was a brusque monkey-faced man with a graying crew cut and an air of impatient kindness. He had evidently been acquainted with the nature of Barney's accident; he shot Kate a glance at once interested and impartial. To Mrs. Maynard, who would have preceded him up the stairs, he said firmly, "I'd rather see the boy alone, if you don't mind, Mrs. Maynard. Now and then, in a case like this—"

Upstairs, the door of Barney's bedroom closed. Kate sat down uncertainly on the edge of the flowered chair, and it was just as hard as it had been yesterday. Across from her, Maynard was like a rather handsome bull: face all

glistening planes and knots, with an upthrust of cheekbones that made crescents out of his surprisingly tender-
looking gray-blue eyes, and a forgotten spill of short black
curls in the middle of his forehead. Beside him, his wife
looked faded and used and angry. Presently they began a
conversation that excluded Kate.

"How do you feel, hon?"

"Oh—" Mrs. Maynard gestured, indicating that her husband ought to know.

"Get in touch with your brother?"

"He's at Webb's Beach with Myrtle. Her mother's still
bad."

There was a pause, while Kate memorized her hands.
Footsteps clumped overhead—the doctor rounding Barney's
bed?—and Mrs. Maynard said nervously, "He was so good
about Barney's tonsils."

"And when he had measles, remember?"

"A hundred and five for two days."

They both shook their heads. It was only natural that
they should be absorbed in themselves and their worry,
Kate told herself, but she had to force down a tiny resentment. They had asked her here, and now they were
making her an intruder—or perhaps they were only trying
to keep from themselves the length of the doctor's stay upstairs. Whatever the injury, it had to be temporary; no
concussion or depth of shock could leave a child permanently mute . . . could it?

To her horror, dampness flashed over her at the thought,
and when she lifted her gaze from the hands clutching
her straw bag the room slipped infinitesimally. Suppose it
should actually topple, suppose she should see the rug
blurring up to meet her? I can't fall, thought Kate wildly,
not here. She pressed her knees tightly together and twined
her wet fingers, and very slowly control began to come
back.

The Maynards watched her with open curiosity. "It's
hot, isn't it?" said Kate idiotically, and upstairs the door of
Barney's bedroom opened.

33

"—and next time I come I want that bird talking too, hear?" The brusque voice echoing down the stairs sounded so very genial and unworried that Kate, with her new knowledge of the medical world, flinched inwardly. But there was nothing to be told from the doctor's face when he walked rapidly down the stairs and into the living room, making himself very busy over the lighting of a cigarette.

"He'll be all right," he said, but after a sharp look at Mrs. Maynard's face his glance went to the man's and stayed there. "I want X rays, and then—do you have hospitalization?"

Kate shrank even afterward from the scene that followed. The doctor explained that the nervous system was a very delicate and sometimes unpredictable mechanism; jar it badly, physically and emotionally, and you could get complicated results. Various control centers . . . That was why he wanted X rays, and a period of observation.

It the midst of this, Mrs. Maynard appeared almost literally to fly apart. Voice breaking hysterically, she cried that her baby would not go to a hospital, her father had just died in one, she knew how they were run. Barney couldn't talk, couldn't ask for anything, couldn't even cry . . .

For Kate, it was shrivelling. She could only command her tongue when Mrs. Maynard, resisting the doctor's low-voiced suggestion of a sedative, said tensely, "—and the money. Where are we to find the money? Jim's been out of work for weeks, we barely get by on unemployment as it is. Show him the bills, Jim, show him—"

"I can help," said Kate in a voice she barely knew. "I'd be glad to, so please don't worry about that."

A little over half an hour later at the bank, she paid a thousand dollars into the Maynards' account.

It was not a particularly easy thing to do, from a financial point of view. Robert had put money into land, and like most men of thirty-six he had not left a large estate. Kate's protracted stay in the hospital, and the expenses of

34

Georgia's patient sojourn in Arizona and their return East —had eaten surprisingly into what there was.

Anything else, however, was unthinkable, especially after her brief talk with the doctor in the driveway. Having given Mrs. Maynard a sedative, he was on his way back to his office to make arrangements for the X rays. When Kate said tightly to him, "Will he really be all right?" he shrugged.

"Probably. I'm not a specialist. God knows, though, Mrs. Maynard can't take care of him herself. She's—well, you saw. I know of a crackerjack nurse, a therapist really, but —" he shrugged again "—they can't afford to work for nothing. Why do these things always happen to people up against it?"

He seemed to remember then who Kate was, and as he got into his car he said with an awkward brusqueness, "Don't blame yourself, Mrs.—Barlow? Obviously the police don't."

He of all people would understand why Maynard had tried to keep his wife from finding out any of this in the beginning. Kate said, "Well, as a matter of fact, I—" and stepped back with a sharp flicker of fear as a butterfly danced past her face. The tiny interruption was fatal to her small attempt at courage. "—I can't help feeling very badly about it," she said.

In less than twenty-four hours, she had taken her second dangerous step.

From the bank, Kate proceeded to Carpenter's, although by this time, unfairly, she would have liked to hurl his manuscript into the nearest pond. It seemed hours since she had prepared herself for his noticing eyes, and in the steamily hot car she could feel her dress sticking to her and her well-brushed hair disintegrating into untidy points and wisps. If only she could go straight home, take a shower, sort out in solitude what this whole terrible business might be going to mean . . .

But she could not. It wasn't far to the lane where Carpenter lived, not more than a mile or so of twists and turns, but in that distance Kate managed to meet a police cruiser. It was pure chance, of course, but she tightened her grip on the wheel and concentrated on driving such a straight sedate line that the nose of the car began to waver instantly.

The cruiser slowed as it approached—to identify her license plate?—and Kate, heart pounding, stopped as the two cars drew abreast and rolled her window down. ("Mrs. Robert Barlow? We have a complaint . . . failure to renew your driver's license . . . failure to report an accident . . . have you ever been involved in an accident before?")

The policeman smiled at her damp flushed face. "You'll roast in there," he observed, and then, "Would you happen to know whether a Mr. Rufus O'Connor lives around here?"

"O'Connor," repeated Kate weakly. "No, Officer, I'm sorry, I don't."

He drove off a moment later with a small friendly salute. Kate turned a deaf ear to the monitor in her own mind that inquired detachedly, Is this the way you mean to live? and continued on her way.

The small, blue-shuttered white cottage at the end of the lane was not really Carpenter's; he was minding it for an aunt of his, abroad for the summer. It had suited him very well, as he was working on a book of his own while he ghosted the manuscript Kate was typing, until he had discovered that he was expected to take personal and detailed care of Mrs. Tellier's flowers. Thunder-faced, he had read to Kate an excerpt from a letter newly arrived from Rome: "And how are my dear petunias? I see their frilly faces . . ."

As Kate turned into the drive she saw that Carpenter had changed his tire and was now laboring discouragedly among the petunias; the net effect was that of a large dog having passed speedily through. He was being ostentatious about having lost a morning's work—but as she crossed the lawn he only straightened to his easy height and said by way of greeting, "Their frilly faces look a tri-fle wrinkled."

"You're supposed to pinch those off. I'm sorry if I've held you up on this."

"I was stuck anyway," said Carpenter, as airily as though he had not prodded her about it that morning. "What would you say to a glass of iced coffee?"

That, of course, out of deference to what must be her flushed and frantic appearance. Kate said to the casual but noticing blue gaze, "Thanks, but I have to be getting back, so if you have no more copy for me . . ."

Odd, but she had never noticed before what a wealth of bees and wasps were concentrated around this small lush lawn and garden. The bees were on a legitimate er-rand, but the tawny circling wasps were not. Kate stood in the deep shade of a maple tree, feeling somehow safer there, and was grateful when Carpenter strolled with her through the sunlit spaces to the car.

He said as he opened the door for her, "How goes the war against Mr. Symmes?"

Like Kate, he evinced only a mild amusement, it was difficult to be censorious about a campaign conducted with such candid indignation. Kate said lightly, "As of yester-day, Mr. Symmes was forging slightly ahead," and got into the car.

The rolled-up window was like a statement of insanity on such a day. Kate rolled it nonchalantly down, keeping a hand watchfully in position, and asked carelessly, "What do you spray for wasps?"

One of Carpenter's virtues was unsurprisableness; if you asked him where you could buy a stuffed ocelot, or if it were possible to attend a beheading, he would merely pause and think. He said now, "A solution of fifty per cent DDT, I think. I've never tried it, but somebody must have told me that."

He looked so reliable, leaning there against the car, that Kate nearly told him: nearly said, "What shall I do?" But it did not become widows to thrust their problems upon unattached men; it seemed to establish some sort of claim.

"Thanks, I'll try it," she said, and as explanation, "it seems so waspy at this time of year."

They gave each other small waves as she pulled out of the driveway—light, friendly but businesslike. Just as it should be. Kate did not see Carpenter's savage kick at the petunias. She drove home in her travelling furnace feeling oddly restored, which was just as well because the thing —she could only call it a thing—came by mail the next morning.

V

THE mail delivery at Ridge Road was nothing short of mischievous. Ten-thirty was the expected time of arrival, but often it did not come until twelve. Anyone relying upon this grace period to get a letter ready for collection was apt to find, however, that the mailman had shot past at nine.

On this particular morning he came early, at about nine-thirty. Kate had spent a restless and broken night, falling into an exhausted sleep at dawn, and she was pouring tomato juice while Georgia sipped at a second cup of coffee.

Even after months, and with most of her mind elsewhere, Kate was still fascinated by her mother-in-law's early-morning appearance. It was not, with Georgia, a hasty matter of towel and toothbrush, lipstick and comb. Creams went on, and astringents, and finally a delicate but full battery of makeup—powder-base, powder, rouge, the lightest touch of eyebrow pencil and mascara—so that although she was usually wearing a robe and old scuffs, her face might have been out at cocktails.

Joanna came in, dropping a sheaf of letters on the table. "Bills," she said succinctly, "and a wedding present we'll have to buy, and some more of those interminable coupons for Boxholder. Oh, and something for you, Kate."

Kate drank her tomato juice and picked up the letter. Georgia had opened the wedding invitation; she said musingly, "Well, for heaven's sake, Madge Perlmutter is getting married."

"At last," said Joanna.

"Ingham . . . I wonder if those are the people who had the yacht here last summer?"

Kate's envelope seemed empty at first, but it was not. A very small newspaper clipping had slid down into the bottom. After a bewildered glance at one side, part of an advertisement for electric scissors, she turned it over. The brief item, under the headline "Wasp Sting Fatal," struck her as hard as a flung stone.

"A Trenton, N.J., woman died yesterday as the result of being stung by a wasp. Mrs. Horace DeJong, 40, was potting plants when her cry attracted the attention of a neighbor. By the time aid was summoned, Mrs. DeJong had lapsed into unconsciousness and was dead on arrival at a local hospital."

Kate's stomach turned slowly, her face grew hot. She glanced at the envelope again, and it was really for her—as if there had been any doubt: Mrs. Robert Barlow, at this address. The handwriting looked merry and unreal, like the flourishes of a child rebelling against prim school script, but this was not the work of a child.

Maynard—or Mrs. Maynard, pale red-rimmed eyes flashing as she combed through old newspapers for an item she remembered reading, idly at the time . . .

Gradually, Kate realized that on the other side of the table Georgia and Joanna had stopped their tactful mumbling about Madge Perlmutter and were watching her bent head and the hand that had gone automatically to the hair over her right temple. Wordlessly, she slid the clipping across.

Georgia said, "What . . . ?" and turned it over, to be confronted by the chopped-off panegyric on electric scissors. The tiny pucker between her eyebrows smoothed as she read the clipping again. "Did you know this Mrs. DeJong?"

"I've never heard of her."

"Somebody thought you had," said Joanna decisively, "or got you mixed up with another Barlow. It's a common enough name."

Yes, thought Kate—if Mrs. DeJong had married her

eighth husband, or been arrested for disturbing the peace, or elected president of the local dachshund club. But a Mrs. DeJong stung to death by a wasp . . .

No one mentioned the possibility of a joke, in bad taste but still intended as such. But then no one mentioned the Maynards either. Looking cool about it, Kate crumpled the clipping and the envelope, poured herself a cup of coffee, and asked Joanna if it was hot out. She thought that both other women looked relieved, as though they were saying to themselves, "Thank heavens, Kate isn't going into a tailspin."

She got her coffee down, just.

The Maynards, certainly, but why? A bitterly hopeful, "This could happen to you"? A statement that no matter what happened she must be haunted by how she had nearly killed their child?

In the apartment, Kate did what she ought to have done earlier: she telephoned the Barlows' doctor. Consultations, or second or even tenth opinions, must be common in situations like this. She did not care much for Patwick, who had appeared to think in her single visit to him that she was malingering, but he seemed a man of probity.

Dr. Patwick would be on vacation for another two weeks. Would Kate care to contact Dr. Morgan, who was taking his calls?

Dr. Morgan was foreseeably busy. An emergency, his nurse inquired—someone, her tone implied, whose head was hanging by a shred? Oh, a second opinion in a case already attended by another doctor . . . she was afraid not, at least until after the fifteenth. Kate might try Dr. Huckabee.

Kate hung up, defeated, because she knew Dr. Huckabee by rumor. No tonsil or adenoid or appendix was safe from him, and he was reputed to shake his head gravely over a hangnail and order a complete set of X rays. The town had not yet become fashionable, and with the exception of an obstetrician and a chiropodist, this completed the medical roster.

So that Dr. Sanderson-Pendleton-Henderson must have his office in Bridgeport. He had been accommodating to make the drive, but then he had evidently been the family doctor for some time. Balked without a Bridgeport directory, Kate lit a cigarette and stared into space.

Almost unwillingly came the knowledge that there was something she didn't entirely like about the Maynards. Not that liking entered into it. The were not after all friends, to be measured in her own terms; they were people thrown into frantic worry because, with a conjunction of time and place so exact that it might have been plotted on a graph, a wasp had flown at a total stranger.

. . . The wasp. How terrifying that a single sting could kill; it must happen once in several million instances. Mrs. DeJong had probably had a heart condition, unmentioned in the brief newspaper account, or an extreme allergy to that particular type of venom. (Outdoors potting plants, exposed to anything that flew?) As with any venom, terror would accelerate its course through the blood stream . . .

Kate's own heart had begun a thicker, faster beat; her muscles jerked involuntarily as something crawled across the sunlit floor of the sitting room. But it was only the shadow of something, a large bee or a wasp feeling its delicate-legged way up a screen, blindly patient, seeking entry. As she watched, the shadow slipped, blurred, circled, and began its tireless trip again.

Kate Barlow is in there.

Kate jumped to her feet, panicky; this was the way people's minds began to warp. And it was precisely what the Maynards, one or both of them, had intended: a new and terrified awareness of this particular part of the insect world, a horror that kept no hours because a wasp warmed and enlivened by electric light was just as active as a wasp in the noonday heat.

Without looking back, she went into the bedroom and made her bed, washed a pair of stockings, tidied up generally. She thought with a little stir of anger that some-body might have let her know the outcome of Barney's X rays. They had made it clear that she was involved; that, rather than the money, gave her the right to know. If no one had phoned by noon, she would call the May-nards, putting out of her mind the thought of a napping child or an hysterical woman summoned out of sleep—

While Kate was making up her mind to that, the door knocker fell.

It was Georgia, unaccustomedly terse. "Mr. Symmes just called, he's bringing someone to lunch. Thank God there's enough chicken left, and Joanna's making salad. Do you think you could . . . ?"

Although it had only happened once before in her stay here, Kate reacted like a member of the ladies' drill team. It was all so savingly ridiculous: the portrait of Mr. Symmes in a celluloid collar and the wedding picture of Gerald and Joanna snatched out of the top drawer and hastily propped up. Mr. Symmes' anniversary gift, a large, ugly hand-painted bowl, placed prominently on the coffee table. A pair of Gerald's slippers, abandoned long ago, allowed to peep out from under the double bed. Unless Mr. Symmes or his com-panion were very prying indeed, there was nothing to be-tray that the apartment was tenanted by Kate.

On the lawn, she passed Joanna, who said only, "The butter knives are in the top left-hand drawer of the buffet."

Whenever he descended, and at whatever short notice, Mr. Symmes was not a man to be fobbed off with a sand-wich or anything else casual; he expected butter knives, water goblets, and linen napkins. He got them. When Kate arrived in the kitchen, Georgia, skin delicately pearl-ed, was trying to get a casserole into the oven and peel an avocado at the same time. She said distractedly, "Would you take this—no, set the table first. The butter knives . . ."

Kate set the table, sliced the avocado, and got the

kitchen in order while Georgia vanished upstairs to refurbish herself. She was barely in time when she descended; a long important car just drawn into the driveway disgorged Mr. Symmes and a woman who turned out to be the dangerous Mrs. Holden.

Gerald's father had never been a large man, and age and vanity had shrunk him so that he always looked to Kate like an escaped and extraordinarily clever monkey. Small as she was on her plump little feet, his companion topped him by several inches. Kate did not mind the plummily dyed hair, or the shrewd avaricious eyes; at the doting, "And that's the apartment you gave them! Caspar, you never told me how charming! Really, they live like kings, but I'm sure they're very grateful," she was solidly on the Barlows' side.

After a cocktail, over which he remarked slyly that it was a pity Gerald's brief lunch hour prevented his joining them, Mr. Symmes attacked his meal as though his emaciation were the result of not having eaten in several weeks. Across from him, Mrs. Holden seemed to see nothing but a mass of unwelcome calories. Presently, with a limpid air, Georgia drew from her the information that she had twin grandchildren—"I was scarcely more than a child myself when I married"—and further, that she always had them with her for holidays.

"Twins must be rather a handful," remarked Georgia dulcetly, not looking at Mr. Symmes.

"Oh, no. You see, they're Loved," said Mrs. Holden, tipping her head significantly, "and all any child needs is Love. And, of course, the freedom to be *itself*."

She did not observe the ominous darkening of Mr. Symmes' face; it was his contention that this school of thought had made a shambles of Gerald. She walked deeper into the trap, her tone earnest, and Mr. Symmes said suddenly and savagely, "Bunch of silly hens," and stabbed at a slice of avocado as though he intended to kill it.

Mrs. Holden, not connecting this with herself, only threw

him an absent smile and blundered on about the dangers of discipline. "Violence never taught anything, whereas a little hug, a bounce on the knee—"

Mr. Symmes' napkin went crashing into his plate. "Lot of—" In his rage, he could not get it out. "Lot of damned—"

Solicitously, Joanna handed him a glass of water. Kate, who had watched it all with a kind of detached admiration, went stiff as the telephone rang.

There were times when the sound seemed to contain a name, and this was one of them. She forced herself to sit still and even smile soothingly at Mr. Symmes while Joanna crossed to the telephone, said, "Hello? Yes, just a minute, please," and then, "It's for you, Kate."

This, and not the airy game the Barlows had just played with Mrs. Holden, was reality. Kate took up the receiver as though it were a yoke, and a brusque voice said in her ear, "Dr. Sanders, Mrs. Barlow. Did the Maynards phone you about the X rays?"

"No. I've been wondering—"

"Well, they're pretty upset. All that shows up is concussion, not too severe in itself, but the boy's condition is the same. Trauma's a tricky thing, and Mrs. Maynard having herself a nervous breakdown isn't helping much."

Trauma: what a sinister, unexplorable sound it had. Kate's faint animosity departed with a rush: in the thin frantic woman with the trembling hands she saw herself ten months ago. She said, "If there's anything . . ." and heard it trail emptily off.

A child wailed in the background, and Sanders' turned-away voice said something about two-tenths of a c.c., Nurse, and then came bluntly back. "Frankly, Mrs. Barlow, as long as they're in that house I don't think there's much to be done. Mrs. Maynard seems to have had a phobia about the place since her husband lost his job and her father died, and hysteria is communicable. I'd guess that's a good part of the boy's trouble. Well—" the voice grew

45

brisk, finishing-up, the voice of a man who has accepted the fact that he cannot heal all the ills of the world "—as you've taken an interest in the case, I thought you'd want to know."

"Yes . . . thank you, doctor."

Thank you for what? A vision of Mrs. Maynard crying over her silenced son? Of Maynard, awkward in the small blue-walled upstairs room, taking over the nursing duties to keep Barney from retreating deeper into fear? Of the unspeakable hostility they must feel toward Kate? The money would have deepened that, if anything; they would think it a matter of writing a careless check . . .

Luckily, during Kate's short sojourn on the phone, Georgia and Joanna had been occupied with being affable to the vanquished Mrs. Holden—it had been so pleasant, hadn't it—and the party was moving toward the door. Kate went with them out to the lawn. For no good reason she felt safe from wasps in the presence of other people; it was as though she gained some kind of anonymity.

When the car had driven off, Joanna said matter-of-factly, "Well, I think that's that," and then, to Kate, idly curious, "Who was that on the phone?"

The light struck into her eyes for a second before she raised a shielding hand. They were brown, like Robert's; a brown so clear and golden that it looked at times as though something shone behind them.

"Oh . . . about the Maynard boy. He's going to be all right," said Kate.

The evasion astonished her. Shame entered into it, and a sense of guilt, and a childish conviction that the less public notice taken of anything, the more likely it was to go away.

But there was a sensible basis, too. Given the facts to date, Georgia and Joanna, and possibly even Gerald, would leap into action right away, not caring how Kate felt about it. They would get lawyers to demonstrate that she had not been at fault, and that only her consideration for a mother's feelings had kept her from reporting the accident at the time. By the same token, they would have it proved that Mrs. Maynard's disturbed emotional state was already in existence and not to be linked with the accident. They would say that Kate had already provided financial assistance not legally required of her—and, having settled everything to their satisfaction, they would leave her with her own private and undying spectres.

Because she had hit Barney, or Barney's tricycle; there was no getting away from that. If only she could study a slow-motion film of her fatal progress along Maple Avenue, to see how much the wasp entered into it . . . Gerald had been there but if the circumstances seemed to require it Gerald would say cheerfully that Barney Maynard had arrived on the crest of a flood, wearing defective water wings.

Or if only Carpenter had provided her with more copy, something to concentrate her attention on . . .

That day was Kate's first intimation of being a prisoner—in a charming apartment in the summer country-side, where the locks would turn at a touch. She did not want to drive more than was absolutely necessary until her license came, if it came. She rinsed a few drip-dry things and did not hang them out on the line behind the apartment because she was stopped, with her hand on the doorknob, by the occasional caravel wings in the sunniness there. It was not so much a fear of being stung (*wasp sting fatal*); she felt that she could have stood it if someone had told her that at exactly four o'clock every afternoon she was to be stung by a wasp. She would be prepared for it then, and the pain was easily bearable.

It was the element of surprise, learned in all its horror from the episode in the car. The sudden dry rasp of wings —or, worse, the random glance at arm or shoulder that would discover the infinitely delicate prowling of jointed legs, the decision still to come: crawl on under the sleeve or the neckline or the hem, or fly harmlessly away, or sting—*here!*

I will have to go to a doctor, Kate thought lucidly. I can't, no one could, live like this.

She could only make a pretense at dinner that evening. Georgia remarked upon it, in her soft but implacable voice. "Don't you feel well, Kate?"

"Large lunch," explained Kate with an effort at nonchalance.

"Mrs. Holden's thrown her off her feed," said Gerald profoundly, "and no wonder. She's a dreadful woman. Do you know that last Christmas she invited a lot of unsuspecting people and served bran mash or whatever that vegetarian stuff is, shaped like a turkey?"

It made a diversion, for which Kate was grateful; she only caught a flicker of Gerald's olive eye. He had learned this kind of thing, she suspected, as a means of ducking away from the sternnesses of the Barlows; it was entirely possible that Mrs. Holden had done no such thing. But it worked: Joanna said with contempt, "I'm surprised. She looks more like a cannibal than a vegetarian," and Georgia said musingly, "I don't believe I've ever seen hair like that before. What would you call it? Puce? Plum . . .?"

Kate slept badly again that night. She saw the useless tremor along Barney Maynard's throat; she heard Maynard say in a beseeching voice, "Alice, it'll be all right," and in the dream, with tears clamping her own throat, she knew that it would not be all right. Barney would scribble on little pads instead of talking, or use his fingers in a hard-learned sign language, and all because of her.

She woke with her throat aching. The morning was gray and cool and windy; what she had come to think of, in the last seventy-two hours, as unwaspy. At ten o'clock, driven by her thoughts, uncertain as to what she would say, she dialled the Maynard's telephone number.

It didn't answer. That didn't mean that things had taken a turn for the worse, that they had taken Barney back to the hospital, but at eleven Kate tried again. And at twelve. She knew now what she would say: "Do you think it would help if you took Barney on a sort of vacation? My own finances are limited, but I'll do what I can."

She tried again at one, and at two. At two-thirty, with a landscape turned purplish and a mutter of thunder in the west, she got into her car and drove carefully to Maple Avenue.

VI

THE street looked strange without its mask of dappled light; strange and still. Houses Kate had never noticed before seemed to have crept closer to the edges, but of course that was the overcast sky, the stilled branches, her own foolish feeling of being watched. Was raw-nerved Mrs. Maynard frightened of thunderstorms? It was to be hoped not, because this one was coming to a fast black boil. Kate got out of her car to the first rap of rain among the maples.

The milk bottles were there on the step again, but empty this time except for a note furled into the top of one. Kate glanced at it and rang the bell—an automatic gesture, because she had realized by now that the old black Chevrolet was not in the driveway, and an empty house had a certain quality of blankness. Barney was not ill in the usual sense, of course; perhaps they had taken him for a drive or to a movie, in an attempt to coax his speech.

The sky split above Kate's head, and she ducked instinctively and saw again the note in the milk bottle. No one wrote confidences to milkmen, and with the rain beginning to pelt down she bent and took it out. Her heart rose instantly, because the brisk pencilled printing said, "Please discontinue milk for two weeks."

She simply stood there a minute, getting progressively drenched, not caring in her relief. They had had the same thought as she and gone away somewhere, removing Mrs. Maynard from the scene of her hysteria, putting behind

Barney a place of fear, and possibly unlocking his tongue. Two weeks wasn't long, but it might be long enough—

The landscape leaped whitely around her, there was the torn-canvas prelude to a crackling roar of thunder. Kate turned and ran through the rain to her car.

The heat returned, and broke records that week. Georgia basked in it like a gratified lizard, Joanna grew browner and thinner, Gerald devised new means for appearing to toil at the plant while he did nothing. Kate did not hear from the Motor Vehicles Bureau, but she did not get any more clippings either. Little by little, the Maynards lost their piercing edge. It was not that Kate felt less responsible; they had simply moved to an unknown area where her imagination could not follow them with such painful exactitude.

Paradoxically, her fear of wasps grew instead of lessening. A moth fluttering behind a curtain, an over-exuberant housefly, even the uncrinkle of balled cellophane carelessly tossed in an ashtray: any of these caught her breath and brought her head flashing around in the direction of the sound. There was no concealing it, not after a yellow jacket pursued her to the door of the house and, in her frantic urgency to get in, she pulled the screen door slashingly shut on three fingers of her left hand.

Georgia said in her soft relentless way, "Really, Kate, you must—"

"—not give in to anything so childish," said Kate, interrupting. She was shocked at her own tone, but she could not seem to help it. "I'm not really enjoying it either, Georgia, much as I may appear to."

"Of course you're not," said Georgia gently. "But don't you think—now don't misunderstand me, Kate—that it might do you good to be stung?"

Stung. The single thump of recognition from her heart, then the stoppage, then the dangerous race . . . "Probably," said Kate, voice still tight and even, "but I don't intend to find out if I can help it. I'm sorry, and I'll get over this,

51

but couldn't you all just—look the other way when I'm making a fool of myself?"

She knew as she said it that she was being both ungrateful and unfair; public flinchings were hard to overlook, and they had all nursed her so patiently over her car phobia, after Robert's death, that she could understand their weariness at another. But even though she addressed herself with far more scorn than they did, the fact remained: it was as useless to tell her not to be afraid of wasps —not to rush through doorways, or turn in a whirl, with her hands pressed blindly against her cheeks—as it was to tell Gerald not to sneeze at goldenrod or cat hair.

It would pass. It had to.

Sternly enjoined by both his wife and his mother-in-law, and prudently wearing a borrowed bee-veil, Gerald went in search of wasp's nests at nearly dusk one evening. He made no pretence of dauntlessness, saying with an unnerved little laugh, "Couldn't you have found someone fonder of wasps?" but he was armed with a kerosene-soaked cloth and a box of matches.

Kate watched him from the apartment with a queer transference of fear. With the going of the sun, the wasps would have retreated to their nests—and be there in force, a seething, constantly-moving mass that did not bear thinking about. Gerald, in the watery gray light, was like some menacing creature from another planet, blind-faced, huge-headed as he walked along a distant line of bushes that grew thickly along a small ditch at the back of the Barlow property.

Was it too dark to see . . . ? No, because he had made a gingerly reconnaissance earlier and a sudden triumphant flame bloomed through the dusk. Against it she could see Gerald duck his head and begin to run.

A feeling of security stayed with her almost all the next day, until there was a sudden dry buzzing from inside the lilacs at her front door and Kate felt, or imagined, a breathlike touch on her hair. Without stopping to think, she struck at the place so violently that she was dizzied;

for an alarming second or two her head rang. It cleared, and Joanna was crossing the grass, her pointed face amused and exasperated. "For heaven's sake, Kate! After all, Gerald burned the nest."

Kate nodded tersely in the direction of the lilacs. "That one was out late," she said.

In a short span of days, her life had changed dramatically. She had stopped wearing any kind of cologne and changed to a scentless soap, because fragrance attracted bees and where you found bees you very often found wasps. She went out in the early mornings or the shadow-hung afternoons, avoiding the quiet sunny midsection of the day. She drove only when absolutely compelled to. Once, when Joanna was out and Georgia remembered something forgotten on the shopping list, she pleaded a bad headache; at another knock, she flung on her robe and said apologetically that she was just about to step into the shower.

If she rose at eight o'clock, this regime left her with over eight hours to fill. With Carpenter apparently mired in his book and no copy to type, she cleaned the spotless apartment, read a great deal, and played endless games of solitaire in which, if she did not get a certain number of cards out, she would have to pay a hair-raising forfeit.

After that first night Georgia had not offered sleeping pills, and, grimly, Kate did without them. She also did without a good deal of her sleep. Her eyelids grew more delicate and noticeable, and belts she had worn at the third notch went into the fifth. All her useless time-killing occupations gave her time to think, and she thought not only about Barney Maynard but, inevitably, Robert.

It would once have seemed impossible to her that such a scene would blur, but it had; or perhaps there were too many other scenes piled on top of it. If she were not absolutely sure whether or not Robert had dozed for a second behind the wheel, mustn't that mean that her eyelids had fallen, too—warned as she was, aware of his fatigue? If she had said decisively, "Robert? No, I won't wait, let's change over, right here," might he still be alive?

The wonder dropped on her like water on stone, ceaseless and hollowing. When Carpenter called one morning and asked casually if she were free for dinner, it was like an oar flung to someone drowning. Or so Kate thought until she discovered that the others had been invited to something connected with Madge Perlmutter's belated engagement. She knew the burden she was in cases like this, with strangers who didn't know of her existence; she had heard more than once Georgia's deft, "Oh, and have you met my daughter-in-law? Yes, Kate's with us now . . ."

But they need not have called Carpenter on this occasion. Angrily, Kate put on a very pale pink sheath of a dress that should have fought with her caramel hair but did not. She was finished with dressing for Carpenter as though he were someone rare and special, someone who must be guarded against.

With the decision, she armed herself all over again, although at the restaurant, a pleasant one with low lights and good but unobtrusive service, Carpenter was easy and companionable. He said that he had gotten his ghosted hero out of a Canadian lumber camp and into the front office by means of a savage black bear, and, when Kate asked warily if there had really been a bear, "All lumber camps are totally surrounded by bears."

His gaze swept over her in a detached, friend-of-the-family examination. "What's happened to you, Kate?"

How much had they told him? Kate was used by now to being discussed—that was the price of sanctuary—but she managed to give him a look of surprise. "Nothing."

"Oh? You look," said Carpenter bluntly, "the way you did when you came back from Arizona."

. . . Back from Arizona. Back without Robert, her future abruptly emptied like a basin, trying to live up to the Barlow strength . . . The restaurant slipped a little, the pink dress was suddenly a sheath of dampness. Kate had to stare at the cigarette in her left hand to realize that her

54

fingers were holding it; her right wandered automatically to her hair. From very far away Carpenter said gently, "Kate."

She had to lift her gaze gradually, so that the table would not tilt. This made . . . how often? Three times in ten days . . . "Take some of your drink," said Carpenter's quiet voice, and she raised the glass obediently. The iciness of the drink as well as the stimulant seemed to restore her balance; Carpenter was all at once the proper distance away, the table was perfectly steady, her fingers know the texture of cigarette paper again. She said with an effort of lightness, "I'm never much good in the heat—will it ever break, do you suppose?"

Carpenter accepted that casually. "They say tomorrow . . ."

All through dinner, he led her through neutral, no-strain subjects: people they both knew, the unplumbable mystery of most best-sellers, a cat of his acquaintance who ate green peppers, fastidiously spitting out the seeds. Over coffee he said in the same negligent tone, "Have you ever thought of getting a regular job?"

Kate gazed at him blankly. "Here in town?"

"Well, no—I don't suppose you know how to make sodas and I'm sure you wouldn't take to measuring ribbon. I meant New York."

"With an hour and a half's commuting? Thank you, no."

"In New York," said Carpenter mildly, "they've come a long way. They have places called apartment buildings, some of them quite pleasant."

In a flash, Kate saw her security ripped from her like a bandage from an unhealed wound, competent strangers measuring her incompetence, a fast cold gray pace carrying her to places she did not want to go. She said flatly, "No," and then, her face burning suddenly, "Did—is this Georgia's idea?"

"No," said Carpenter. "Poor, apparently, but my own. Benedictine? No? . . . You don't seem to realize the extent of my unselfishness." His eyes were grave. "To find someone literate, who can read my writing, type beautifully, look—"

"I think I've dropped a glove," said Kate rapidly, and thought with irrelevance as he bent how disarming his hair was, as smooth and innocent and light-brown as a child's. She couldn't have said why it always took her by surprise.

A strangeness had sprung up between them, and they drove back to the house in silence. The others were still out. Kate had forgotten to leave a lamp burning in her apartment, and the windows looked black and sly in the glitter of Carpenter's headlights, almost as though they had succeeded in sucking something in out of the night. She was grateful when Carpenter said matter-of-factly, "I'll just see you in."

But the lamps, when she found them, lit up only serenity: the covered typewriter on its table in the corner, the book face down on the couch; in the bedroom, her robe a splash of blue over the foot of the bed where she had tossed it after her shower.

Something hummed, but that was the electric clock. Something rustled dryly—Carpenter, who smoked too much, had just opened a pack of cigarettes. Kate's harshly-caught breath, not quite a cry, checked him at the door. She rushed blindly into him; her muffled voice said against his tie, "On the lamp by the couch—"

It was a very large yellow-jacket, enlivened by the warmth of the bulb, crawling hungrily up the shade, seeming to Kate's wild gaze to plough with its feet at the textured fabric. When Carpenter advanced on it with a rolled magazine it shot obliquely to the ceiling directly over where she crouched against the door, buzzed angrily there, and fell almost at her feet.

Carpenter's shoe covered it instantly, but there was a faint sick pain in the very center of her chest. Not imaginary; she could locate it with her fingers, press on it, feel it ebb. Had Mrs. DeJong felt like this when she saw

56

the delicate brown body, too late, winced under the vicious thrust?

Carpenter's face looked shaken. He said slowly, "Kate dear . . ." and Kate's defenses went crumbling. She said almost in a whisper, "Well, you see. Do you think—no, don't, I mean this seriously—do you think I could be on the way to losing my mind?"

VII

KATE had expected to lie awake. Instead, she slept like someone stunned. Part of that was a catching-up on the last few broken nights; part was Carpenter's rough "Don't talk nonsense!" to her desperate query.

He knew about her driving accident, Joanna had told him. He said sensibly, "If a robin had flown at your windshield you'd hate robins for a while, even though the boy's all right. I gather you're not—involved with these people in any way?"

So many lies to undo, so many puzzled frowns to face —Kate was too nervous and too tired to argue the thousand dollars, and already she had begun to feel that by flying to him for protection she had somehow handed herself to Carpenter, unasked. She said elliptically, "They've gone away for a while," and he looked relieved. He made a thorough inspection of the apartment, and at the door he said, examining the knob, "Go to a doctor, will you?"

"A regular doctor, you mean?"

"Certainly," said Carpenter crossly. "You've lost weight, in case you haven't noticed, and you are as jumpy as a witch. Maybe vitamins, or tranquilizers—"

And maybe they would, thought Kate as she got ready for bed; maybe it was something as simple as that, the physical part of it anyway. She had a distant cousin with hypoglaecemia, and the symptoms of dizziness were remarkably similar. When Dr. Patwick got back from his vacation she would . . .

Sleep took her then, and held her until—who knew

exactly how long before waking? In a vivid dream she was out on the angle of grass behind the apartment when she saw in the sunlight something that looked at first like a small bird. But it was not, it was a cluster of wasps locked together in a fuzzy brown broadened Y, drifting lazily but purposefully toward her. She knew that she would not survive if it caught her, and there was no time to run. She flung herself flat in the shadowed grass, shielding her head with her crossed arms, and woke with her face plunged into the pillow and her heart thundering.

When the mail came that day there was a letter for Kate, postmarked Bridgeport.

Joanna said of her mail, "Shepherd's has a sale of English china that might be worth looking into." Gerald, examining a Brooks ad, said to no one, very thoughtfully, "Would you like me in a vest?" Georgia read aloud an invitation to a tea for Madge Perlmutter, and under the sheer pressure of events, fighting an instinct toward secrecy, Kate opened her letter.

It was typed, which surprised her until she looked at the signature, "J. Maynard," in the sharp shaken hand of someone unfamiliar with a pen. It was also full of queerly archaic misspellings and capitals.

"Dear Mrs. Barlow: I don't know wether you know we have moved, my Wife was in very bad nervus shape and couldn't stand the house. I thought you would like to know that Barney is better now only he has a terrible Stutter. Also he can not remember being hit. We are staying with my Wife's brother, he is a forman here and will try to get me a job. Very truly yours, J. Maynard."

The simplicity of it caught at Kate's heart. And the stammer: her father's speech had faltered after a stroke, and she could still remember the delicate agony of standing in his bedroom doorway, tray-laden, fearful of looking either patient or impatient while his tongue struggled.

She said to the expectant silence, "The Maynards have

moved," and Georgia said placidly, "There, you see? I told you they wouldn't dare try to hold you responsible. When I hit the horse that time—"

Joanna cut across that, pouring coffee for herself and Gerald. "Have they moved permanently, or do they say?"

"I gather it's a matter of his finding work."

"There are lots of jobs in Bridgeport," said Joanna coolly. "Who knows, it may be a blessing in disguise."

Kate felt an actual flash of nausea. Gerald said deprecatingly, "Personally, I like my blessings a little less disguised. Coffee, Kate? That must be cold."

Kate tipped her coffee into the sink and refilled her cup. Gerald had brought in the mail. How sharp-eyed of Joanna to have read the Bridgeport postmark. . . .

Carpenter's book proceeded, for which Kate was grateful. They were punctiliously shy of each other since the evening when she had taken shelter against his chest, and when he gave her the copy he said only, "No rush on this. How are things going?"

"Oh . . . fine."

"Been to the doctor yet?"

"He isn't back from vacation."

"I'm in the wrong business," said Carpenter dryly. "How's Mr. Symmes faring?"

"It depends which side you're on. He seems very much taken with Mrs. Holden."

"God help her," said Carpenter sincerely.

On his remembered advice, Kate went to the hardware store and bought a can of DDT powder and an Army-surplus mask, a gray, snoutlike nightmarish thing. She had asked Georgia's permission to spray the window frames and doorways of the house, too; and new awareness of her own financial status prevented her from calling a man to do it. With a rented pressure sprayer, suspecting the futility of it in a wide country landscape, she proceeded stubbornly around house and apartment, spraying behind shutters as well. That night, as though a mocking

Providence had ordered it, there was a hard sweeping rain.

On the foolish premise that knowledge destroyed fear, she went to the local library and got out a book on insects. After struggling past praying mantises and ichneumon flies she got to wasps (order Hymenoptera) and was horrified to discover that they had biting mouth parts as well as, in the females and workers, formidable stings. She read about the habits of mud wasps and the irritability of white-faced hornets, and when she reached an enlarged drawing of a yellow jacket she closed the book firmly. She had never imagined that tiny harsh furring along the lower legs . . .

Whoever had said that terror lay only in the unknown had never read up on wasps. Now that Kate knew where to look for nests—on woodwork, in certain low-growing bushes, in hollow trees or suspended from branches—she felt doubly exposed in the languid summer landscape. And how that was extolled in song and story, especially the "bee-loud glade." Obviously there were people walking around as free as air who liked that concentrated humming, found it soothing and innocent and pleasant.

As though to underline the irony of this, on the first Wednesday in August, in another of the merrily-addressed empty-seeming envelopes from Bridgeport, came another newspaper clipping. Kate knew roughly what it would say, but her midriff still went hollow at the small-point headline: "Bees Kill Child."

The story had an Ohio dateline. "A four-year-old girl was stung to death by swarming bees near a farm in outlying Briarly today. Playmates reported that Mary Dvorsky . . ." Kate crumpled the clipping savagely without reading any more, but that did not shut out a vision of small terrified girl fleeing from a cloud of humming darkness.

It was the kind of coverage used for bottom-of-the-column filler in almost every daily newspaper. How accomplished Mrs. Maynard's eye must be by now, skipping the average life span of the platypus and the population of

61

Peru in 1911, stopping only on key words: *wasp, bee, sting*. Because it was certainly Mrs. Maynard who, with or without her husband's knowledge and consent, addressed those envelopes. J. Maynard's cramped shaky signature could never have curved and swelled into those carefree loops. Or . . . ?

In her apartment, not even finding it strange that she should be doing it, Kate picked up pen and paper and wrote "Mrs. Robert Barlow" in a number of scripts as different as possible from her own forehand. She had read enough to know the significance of pressure and looped letters and the opening or closing of vowels, and she altered those deliberately. The effect was startlingly alien, and proved nothing at all.

But: "My Wife was in very bad nervus shape."

And was striking out in the most vindictive way she could think of without exposing herself and her child to lawyers, documents, fresh examinations by untrusted doctors. It was almost as though she thought Kate had selected a victim and aimed the car, and must be paid back.

Was Kate, who had recoiled so bitterly when she heard that Robert was dead, and braced herself with terror for so long in even the slowest-moving vehicle—was Kate to sit in judgment?

She understood now the note they had left for the milkman, and the lack of any return address on Maynard's letter. The had not wanted their creditors to know that they were leaving town permanently, and they did not want a collection agent to find them. Again, under the circumstances, who was to moralize about obligations and acting in good faith?

But she grew to dread the mail, and a new fear had been planted as to the legitimacy of bees. Kate had always thought of them as single-mindedly pollinating blossoms or gathering honey, but apparently this was not the case. When they swarmed (and just when did they swarm in this part of Connecticut?) they would strike down anything in their path . . .

Every bee she saw, and in the ripeness of August there were many of them, looked unmistakably like a queen, and two bees looked like the outriders of a swarm.

Dr. Patwick came back from vacation, and Kate went to him.

John Deering Patwick, head of the local hospital, was a man whose very aspect endowed him, and correctly, with quietly perfect antiques, a wife who came from a long line of money, and handsome grandchildren on Shetland ponies. Kate suspected uncharitably that his looks had a good deal to do with his eminence, because if it came to raising funds for a new hospital wing, what wealthy widow could refuse him?

Sitting on the corner of his desk, he listened courteously over folded arms to Kate's description of her dizziness, her inability to sleep, her terror of wasps. She felt her face burn as she came to that; she had known she would feel foolish, but not how foolish.

Dr. Patwick, however, only nodded his tanned blue-eyed face noncommittally. "I see. Well, let's have a look, shall we?"

Heart and lungs and blood pressure, throat and ears and reflexes; at the end of it Patwick said that although if she liked he would make a laboratory appointment for blood-sugar tests he very much doubted hypoglaecemia. He did frown over her weight. He prescribed sleeping capsules and a tranquilizer, and said deprecatingly, "As for the wasp business, I think you're the only one who can help yourself there, don't you?"

"I suppose so," said Kate out of a quiet despair.

"Wasps are unpleasant," conceded Patwick generously. "So are snakes and rats and ticks, but they do exist and there isn't much we can do about it. Frankly, Mrs. Barlow, I think if you were stung a few times you'd lose this . . . phobia."

"Doctor," said Kate in a steady voice, "even when you say that it makes my skin prickle."

Patwick frowned tinily, less out of surprise, Kate felt, than a dislike of any kind of argument. He said pleasantly, "It's been—how long since your husband's death, Mrs. Barlow?"

"Ten months—a little more. But it isn't that."

Patwick smiled. "You think it isn't that." His glance at his watch was as fleeting as a polite hostess's in the presence of an overstaying guest, and as unmistakable; Kate stood up, clutching her gloves. He had already dismissed her from his real attention, but she said anyway, "Is there any preparation I could put on, any repellent . . . ?"

It was a moment or two before Patwick glanced from busily recording her idiocy in a file folder. "I doubt it. In any case, the thing to do is discourage this phobia, not help it along . . ."

Kate asked herself as she left what she had expected, but she knew. She had hoped to be told that her trouble was physical and that an aberration such as hers was common in such cases; that when the condition itself was cleared up, the terror would go with it. Instead, in a flash of panic, she looked forward to a lifetime of this: driving about in sealed-up, boiling-hot cars, feeling her skin pepper with fright at innocent noises, starting violently back at a scrap of dried leaf, a tangle of thread, a grape stem.

Georgia said expectantly at dinner that night, "What did the doctor say?"

Just what you did, that I ought to be stung . . . A childish resentment, plus a firm determination not to see this piece of advice carried out, made Kate reply carelessly, "Oh, nerves, and he gave me some pills. Don't I look tranquil?"

"As a matter of fact, you look quite irritable," said Georgia.

Joanna preserved a tactful but observant silence, and Gerald plunged into the tale of an irritable and successful business acquaintance who, driven to ask his doctor for a tranquilizer, became as mild as milk, lost all his money, and returned to his doctor to beg for pills to make him irritable again.

Georgia listened seriously; like many people who laugh often and effortlessly, she was totally without humor. "How perfectly ridiculous. As though bad temper could be a business asset—!"

I know what I'll do, thought Kate, retreating to her own private world. Even when I'm alone I'll pretend I'm being watched, and that everything hangs on not being found out . . .

And, for a day or two, it worked surprisingly well. When she had to cross the lawn or go out to her car, she kept her vision only on her goal and walked with such purpose that she created an air-clearing draft. She worked zealously at her typewriter, and was careful not to glance at the sunny sheltered windows. If a fold of curtain stirred against the edge of a magazine, or paper settled dryly in a wastebasket, she said aloud, "I wonder what that is?" because she had evolved a theory that sound vibration frightened wasps off.

Of course, she was talking to herself, which was not a particularly comforting realization, but she did very well until an afternoon when there was a sudden heavy hum in the bedroom and she said her usual talisman, "I'll go look," and did.

There above her bureau, apparently believing the mirror to be a window, floated the most enormous thing she had ever seen, furred light brown and black, its drone like a motor. She snatched at the doorknob, and although it slipped from her fingers the stir of air pulled the thing —was it a bee?—toward her. Blindly, forgetting all her resolutions, Kate ran through the living room, wrenched the front door open and escaped, crashing her shoulder hard against the door frame.

She could not measure the effectiveness of the tranquilizer, but the sleeping pills certainly worked. It was an unhealthy sleep, leadenly deep, but it was dreamless and sure. Unfortunately the pills affected her stomach, and after several days of vague nausea she stopped them.

She did not realize, until it came on a morning of pouring rain, that her whole system had been waiting for another communication from J. Maynard.

VIII

THIS letter was longer, oddly capitalled as before and signed with the same squeezed-out "J. Maynard." Kate read it rapidly and then, to the gurgled sound of rain outside the lighted kitchen, re-read the parts that mattered.

"Barney hides from other children because of his Stutter, it is getting worse. He is afraid of bycicles when he sees them on the street but he does not remember why.

". . . My Wife is worse, the doctor says Mellancollia and she should go to a nursing-home as it is bad for Barney. We have to pay my bro-in-law board. They have a boy who makes fun of Barney. If you can help us out until I get work we will be very thankful.

"P.S. If you can send cash because the people around here do not trust checks would you send it to General Delivery so my bro-in-law will not get hold of it."

The kitchen door opened suddenly on glowing rain, and Gerald came in, looking wet and harassed. "Forgot my merit badge," he explained to Kate and disappeared into the inner regions of the house. He came back presently with an imposing leather briefcase which, he confided, contained only blank letterheads, inventory sheets, and some old correspondence filched from the office files for verisimilitude.

"Whenever my father turns up I grub around in it and frown," said Gerald. Kate's motionlessness seemed to register then, and he laid the briefcase down and examined her anxiously. "Something the matter?"

"Oh . . . I keep wondering about—you know, the accident," said Kate. She tried to keep her tone random, so as to get at the truth. "If it hadn't been for the wasp, could I have stopped in time, do you think?"

"No," said Gerald sturdily and without any reflection at all.

"But I wouldn't have been driving that close to the edge if I hadn't had to pull off the road," pursued Kate, relentless with herself, "and if I hadn't braked in a panic that way I might have been able to swerve."

"Nonsense," said Gerald, but his long face showed a flicker of discomfort. "Anyway, I don't see—" His glance fell on the letter under Kate's hand, and the discomfort became alarm. "You don't mean they're talking about suing?"

"No," said Kate, but her heart sank; it was clear which way Gerald thought a suit would go. Not that she hadn't always known—frightened blue-eyed Barney had only to be produced before the court by his frantically haggard mother—but having it confirmed was a little worse, because it bore out her own conviction of her part in the accident.

"Then—?" said Gerald in a puzzled voice, and Kate felt the letter crackle under the involuntary pressure of her hand She said, looking down at it, "They need money."

"Oh," said Gerald profoundly, and sat down across from her, polishing the lock of his briefcase with a bony forefinger Kate realized with a little stab of guilt that she would not have mentioned the letter if the house had not been empty except for the two of them; Georgia was at one of her numerous civic committees, and Joanna was having her hair done.

Rain blinded the windows on a sudden sweep of wind, and Gerald said as though the hiss of it had roused him, "Well, any advice of mine is almost infallibly wrong, but if you do give them money oughtn't you to get a release of some kind? I mean—" his long-lashed olive glance lifted to hers "—this could go on for a long, long time." He looked earnest and concentrating, but Kate could see his mind beginning to ramble in a peculiarly Gerald-like fashion. "I have a vision of him going off to kindergarten and falling off swings, going to elementary school and getting beaned by baseballs, on to high school and football injuries—"

"Stop," said Kate imploringly, and the telephone rang. Gerald seized his briefcase, said rapidly, "I left ten minutes ago," and was gone in a slicing spatter of rain.

The call was for Joanna, and it seemed somehow incredible that it should actually be Madge Perlmutter. Kate wrote the message on a pad beside the telephone—you would never have to hunt for paper or pencil in any household run by the Barlows—washed her cup and saucer, flicked off the kitchen light because Georgia was irritable about the bill, and went out into the rain.

For the first time in weeks she lingered on the lawn; with no one to see her, she stepped out of her sandals and walked barefoot through the wet springy grass. The soaking air was safe, and for a short interval she forgot the letter in her pocket in the pure pleasure of reacquainting herself with sky and wind and vivid dripping green. A sudden vision of coming out only when it rained, like something in a Swiss clock, turned up her mouth-corners in her lifted face—and there all at once, as though he had come out of a crack in the ground, was Carpenter.

How long had his car been there, parked in the very end of the driveway? How long had he watched her amusedly, studying at his leisure her wet hair, her clinging dress, her general air of abandon?

"Hello," said Kate nonchalantly, her face pink under the cool rain, her sandals dangling from one hand.

"I've brought you the rest of the copy. I imagine you'll be glad to see the last of this guy."

For a startled second Kate did not realize that he meant the lumber baron. She said, "I'd better get it under cover," but Carpenter did not relinquish the sheaf of yellow copy paper. Instead, he walked with her to the apartment door and, almost absently, accompanied her inside.

To Kate, the envelope in her pocket seemed all at once very large and noisy. She put the copy beside her typewriter and slid her bare feet into her sandals; only a few blades of grass and clover leaves remained on the rug as mementos of her brief freedom.

"What did the doctor say?" inquired Carpenter.

"Oh—to get a grip on myself."

"How helpful. Patwick, I assume, in his very best imported slacks?"

At Kate's nod he picked up Mr. Symmes' gift bowl, which she had forgotten to put away, looked incredulously at the bottom of it, and put it down again. "Any more wasp trouble?"

The monstrous thing in her bedroom . . . "Very little," said Kate.

"That's one unpublicized advantage about living in New York—no wasps to speak of."

It took Kate a second or two to follow that. "There won't be any wasps here either in a month or so," she said steadily.

Carpenter glanced in silence at her thinned and shadowed face and began to walk idly around the sitting room, flicking up the cover of a magazine, pausing to stare attentively at a small water-color seascape that had hung in Kate's room when she was a baby. He said with his back to her, "You do know, don't you, that they adored Robert?"

After all his idleness and amiability, it fell on Kate like a lash on an unsuspecting back. "Well, of course I . . . naturally they—"

"I don't believe you have any idea at all," said Carpenter quietly, turning to face her. "He was an idol, and nothing less in this family. People who knew them always said God help Robert's wife."

Kate felt like striking him. She said out of a bleak throat, "How nice for them all that they needn't worry now," but Carpenter went on as though he hadn't heard.

"When he married you, from the time they knew he was going to marry you, Georgia made up her mind not to be the general notion of a mother-in-law, and Joanna was handsome enough to withdraw her claim, too. Yes," he repeated to Kate's uncomprehending face, "claim."

It was as though the walls had begun to warp in toward her, destroying every known perspective. Kate felt equally bewildered by what he was saying and the fact that he was saying it at all; she had somehow gone past anger. "Even if all this were true—"

"You know the old saw about losing a son and gaining a daughter-in-law. What I'm getting at," said Carpenter abruptly, "is that I wonder how good this set-up is for any of you—you particularly. You don't appear to be exactly thriving here."

"Just possibly," said Kate, getting her stiff lips open, "running over small children doesn't agree with me. There are people like that."

"And," said Carpenter controlledly, "that was some time ago. Aren't you going to tell me this is none of my business?"

When Kate did not answer he went to the door, turned, said in a driven tone she had never heard from him before, "You don't think I want you to go away?" and walked out into the rain.

When the sound of his car had died away, Kate took Maynard's letter from her pocket and stared blindly at it. "Mrs. Robert Barlow" . . . that, she supposed, was what Carpenter had been fumbling around the edges of: that while she lived here with Robert's mother and sister she had no identity except that. It was not true, she thought sharply; she had . . .

What exactly did she have?

How odd that the rain which had charmed her less than half an hour ago should seem suddenly so grim, curtaining the apartment like mist. Kate looked away from the drop-scribbled windows. She had to think what to do about the Maynards, had to put this new bewildering thing out of her mind.

". . . they adored Robert." Carpenter had implied a

fanatical, almost an unnatural attachment, and Kate did not believe it. If that had been the case, Georgia and Jo-anna would have resented her survival of the accident that had killed him; her very continuing existence, in those first few weeks, would have been a constant reproach. Not even the Barlow discipline could have concealed that.

Still, was it possible that for some unrelated reason Georgia had asked Carpenter to sound her out on the question of moving away? Kate glanced almost wildly around her known, safe shelter. She had a sudden appalling vision of elevators full of staring strangers, crowded subways, res-taurants where you were as conspicuous as an obelisk be-cause you sat alone.

She would have to talk to Georgia. Before that, she had to answer Maynard's letter—or request. (". . . they have a boy who makes fun of Barney.") She had lived so long with Barney's image that it came effortlessly: round blue eyes, round fair head, wary, chiselled littleboy mouth. Kate sat staring at the telephone for minutes on end before she got out the phone book and looked up the number of the local post office.

The bus to Bridgeport two afternoons later was crowded. Kate sat toward the front, trying not to advertise, by her tight grip on her flat straw bag, that she was carrying eight hundred and fifty dollars in cash.

Although the post office had given her mail-delivery in-formation, she suspected that she had very little chance of encountering Maynard at the General Delivery window. He would be anxious about the money, but any number of things might prevent his coming today, the logical date he would expect it if Kate responded promptly. She had ex-plained her position in a letter folded around the bills in the envelope in her bag, but if she could talk to him she would feel surer that she had made it clear. For both their sakes, the Maynards would have to understand that she was at the end of her resources.

She had left her checking account perilously low. When

that was gone there was only the land Robert had left; land-conscious Georgia would buy it happily but Kate had an almost superstitious fear of letting it go. She would have to get a job—but in order to be even halfway employable she would first have to lay this private ghost.

The bus stopped at the post office. Kate shrank from the strange hurrying faces, the onslaught of city heat, the glare that seemed to burst up out of the pavement. She had to force herself up the littered steps and into the building that echoed with the beat of busy heels. Beside the General Delivery window, feeling as spotlit as someone turning over ransom money, she took up her station.

It was four-fifteen, and then four-thirty. At one of the counters a plump hairless young man who had been there when she came in began to stare at Kate; gradually, his face turned knowing. She had arranged some sort of shabby rendezvous, and she had been stood up . . . when her roaming glance caught his he gave her a sly little smile.

Kate's face burned. She turned her head quickly, as though she had just caught sight of a friend, and the post office rocked gently and her palms went wet inside her gloves. Very carefully, keeping her attention on the stitched seams, she took off one glove and put her hand against the cool polished wall. She must not look as though she were going to faint, because that would seem to invite him over. Slowly, under the exertion of her will, the building steadied again and her panic subsided measurably, like water absorbed into sand.

It grew to be five o'clock, and the clerks' windows closed. Kate dropped the envelope containing the money and the letter into the "Local" chute with a feeling of despair: would they really understand? Deliberately, at the door, the hairless young man collided with her. He muttered something about "a show" and "a good time" and Kate ran precipitately toward the knot of people waiting for the 5:10 bus.

Joanna said at dinner that night, "Did you get your teeth cleaned?"

"Yes," said Kate.

IX

IN the normal course of events it was surprisingly difficult
to talk to Georgia alone without making a formal audience
of it. After her early morning coffee she retired to her
desk to take care of bills and correspondence, and it was
understood that she was not to be disturbed at this. Un-
critical of her sex except where Mr. Symmes' dangerous
proclivities were concerned, she enjoyed the society of
other women and belonged to a number of clubs which,
when they were not engaged in something earnest like
petitioning the local authorities to take action about the
water-fountain situation in the tiny town park, held func-
tions called "coffees."

These activities, plus a religious afternoon nap with skin
cream and eye pads firmly in place, took up a large part
of Georgia's day. The cocktail hour was general, and after
dinner she watched television with almost childlike devotion
until nine-thirty, when she went upstairs. Her goodnights
were implacable; it was clear that there would be no
tête-a-têtes in her room.

This evening Kate was in luck. Joanna and Gerald departed to a movie, and, in the living room, Georgia crossed
to the television set and switched it on, saying over her
shoulder, "There's a marvelous play on tonight—I hope I
haven't missed the beginning."

"Georgia," said Kate urgently while the set warmed up,
"if you have just a minute I'd like to—"

"—tender noodles," interrupted the blank screen, "and
oh-so-good golden gravy. Be sure you—" There was a brief

75

flaring glimpse of a man smiling hysterically at a can of soup, and then sound and picture vanished, leaving only a dead façade of wood and glass.

Georgia made a sound of exasperation. "Damn—I told Joanna to call the repair people. Well . . ." She fiddled unavailingly with the knobs, reversed the plug, and gave up. "I suppose that's that."

Kate was startled; it was one of the few times she had ever seen Georgia angered out of her usual placidity, the soft prettiness gone tight, the blue eyes amazingly sharp. It was hardly the best time to broach the subject of the apartment, but she would have difficulty sleeping if she thought the campaign for her removal was inching quietly along.

She said reassuringly that it was probably a small tube, and then, steeling herself, "Georgia, I've been wanting to ask—I should have asked long before this—if you have other plans for the apartment?"

Georgia, who had been resentfully lighting a cigarette, stopped with the waved-out match in mid-air. The irritation vanished from her face, leaving it bewildered. "The —? Your apartment? What in heaven's name put that into your head?"

Kate's flood of relief was almost physically weakening. "Well, it was a temporary arrangement to begin with, and now that I'm better I thought that maybe . . ."

(Only not I, she thought with a strengthening flash of anger: Carpenter. Filtering a kind of ugliness into this house, hoping to infect her with it—why?)

"Kate, you must be mad," said Georgia, and she could not possibly have simulated her distress. "In the first place we love having you here, even if I do feel a little guilty about taking rent. And—well, you really aren't that much better, you know, you haven't looked well ever since that business about the child. Is that what's been worrying you?"

"It hasn't been exactly soothing," said Kate. Sympathy, in her present state, made her voice shake very slightly, but she had to go on; it was like cutting a bad spot out of an apple. "I know the apartment was intended for Joanna and Gerald, and people do change their minds. If they want—"

"Of course they don't," said Georgia at once, but she seemed to remember the dead match in her hand and turned to place it very carefully in an ashtray. Kate felt a flicker along her nerves, because this was exactly Gerald's reaction of the other morning: instant reassurance, and then speculation.

"Joanna feels as I do," said Georgia, firm again, "that the place is yours for as long as you'll stay. You'll have another life some day, of course, but in the meantime —well, heavens, where would Robert's wife be?"

So it was Carpenter, or Carpenter and Joanna between them. Kate was safe, because the decision was Georgia's, and her peace of mind was only faintly flawed by her mother-in-law's terminology. Of course she was "Robert's wife": what else could she possibly mean to the Barlows? Still, she was just as glad that Carpenter had not been there to hear it. She was gladder still, because of the growing awkwardness between them, that another few days would see the end of his book, which the lumber baron wanted to call *Timber! The Story of Virgil Beal Scott.*

As any other random un-personal thing encountered during the day, the name wove ridiculously into her dreams that night. For some reason she had to deliver the finished manuscript to Virgil Beal Scott, but he wasn't home when she got there. She was about to put the box down on his enormous polished desk when the green blotter began a tiny independent crawling movement across the surface. Kate lifted a corner of it, and it was borne on a solid, dully-shining pad of wasps.

Her gasp of horror woke her, and her frantic thrashing in the tangled sheet. She sat up, heart banging; it was moments before the total silence of her own bedroom filtered through to her senses. Could it be good for anybody's heart to beat like that? (Mrs. Horace DeJong . . .)

But Patwick had listened to Kate's heart, even if he had

THE WASP

listened with his mind already made up, his diagnosis arrived at. Presently she lay down again, and as a child
daring disaster along the top of a fence, her mind began
to wonder if wasps could really carry a blotter. Yes, because in the dim days when wasps were only an idle topic
someone had told her of such an experience. It had happened in the early spring, when the dormant wasps had
been warmed to life in a close, low-roofed attic. Probably
their backs were so used to the fuzzed papery shelter that
they had carried it with them—and then what?

Kate had not asked before, nor cared. Now, in the
dark, her brain presented her with the blotter toppling
over the edge of the desk and hitting the floor, the shocked
and enlivened wasps stinging futilely at it and then crawling free, the winged brown progress across the floor and
up the walls . . . Some of them would be flying by now,
blindly and dizzily . . .

She reached for her bedside light, sat up, and read
until a quarter of five, when her weighted eyelids were a
guarantee against dreams. She was correspondingly exhausted when Joanna came to see her a few short hours later.

There were people who seemed at their very best in the
morning, while Kate's metabolism was still trying to find
out where it was, and Joanna was one of them. Clear-eyed
and poised in blade-slim black and white cotton, a supple
turn of gold around one tanned wrist, she came at once
to the point. Georgia had mentioned Kate's qualms about
the apartment, and Joanna was sorry if anything she had
said had given Kate the impression that the place was
wanted.

"Gerald and I far prefer the house. This is fine for one
person, but much too small for a pair of anything but
turtledoves."

Her direct, fringed glance seemed completely open, but
there was something not quite usual about the planes of
her crisp, pointed face. "I do wonder, though, how good
it is for you, staying here."

Kate reached mutely for a cigarette, and her unsteady fingers sent a glass ashtray tumbling from the small table beside the couch. She saw with unnatural fascination that it did not splinter but broke into two perfect shining pieces. It seemed almost an omen, but of what?

"I mean, you see so much of yourself," said Joanna, bending for the ashtray halves as casually as though she had not noticed Kate's utter movelessness. Her thin browned fingers fitted them idly together, with only a twisted gleaming crack of light to show the damage. "But of course you know best about that."

How had Carpenter put it? "I wonder how good it is for any of you . . ." and "Robert was an idol in this family . . ." Kate did not believe it, but what vengeance indeed upon a fate that had allowed Robert's wife to survive him: to give her sanctuary and then expel her from it when she needed it most, kindly but firmly, "for her own good" . . .

Joanna was watching her attentively. "You look fairly frightful, by the way. You don't suppose you're running a temperature?"

"Oh, no. I'm fine," said Kate, and Joanna frowned at her. "Are you taking your sleeping pills?"

"Yes." It was so much easier to lie.

"Well—" Joanna stood up with the sure economy of motion that was so hauntingly reminiscent of Robert; neither of them, thought Kate, suddenly forlorn, had ever bumped against doorways or joggled tables or taken a wrong step anywhere. She was accordingly caught by surprise when Joanna said suddenly, "Can you keep a secret?"

It was not the usual rhetorical prelude to a confidence, and Kate hesitated tinily before she said yes.

"It's really too good not to be shared. We were entertaining Gerald's stepmother at lunch the other day."

Kate was so stunned by the dry crisp words that she had to go groping back. "You mean Mrs. Holden?"

"Mrs. Symmes," corrected Joanna in the same contained voice. "Quite a joke on Gerald and me, wouldn't you say, while we're running about and doing his bidding like good children?"

That, of course, would explain Mr. Symmes' gobbling rage about Love and Freedom: it was his wife speaking, not a female acquaintance who could be hastily discarded. Still, it was difficult to believe such slyness, and at Kate's incredulous expression Joanna said, "Oh, yes, I'm sure. They were married in Vermont in June, and my dear father-in-law attended to changing his will right away. I went to school with Sue Wallace—she'd left Snaith and Snaith to go off and have a baby and came back one day for some stuff she'd left in the office and overheard the new provisions. She had just now," said Joanna with marked grimness, "gotten around to saying isn't it too bad?"

Kate thought she had an inkling of how bad it was. Joanna was undoubtedly fond of Gerald, but it was no secret that the marriage had been based at least in part on his eventual inheritance—and so, logically, was the younger Symmes' credit. Joanna dressed with the beautiful simplicity that always came a trifle higher, and although Kate was not familiar with the cost of men's clothes she suspected that no one with Gerald's odd drooping frame walked in and bought expensive-looking tweeds off a rack.

If the lawyer's ex-secretary were to go around gossiping, mightn't there be a sudden gathering of vultures—and how prepared was Georgia, in charge of the family finances, to assuage them? "The queen was in her counting-house . . ." Did some suspicion of this fought-against development account for Georgia's longer sterner hours at her bedroom desk?

Joanna was turning the slender wrap of gold at her wrist as though she had noticed a flaw in it. Kate said, "Does Gerald know?" and it was not the foolish question it sounded because Joanna's glance came up sharply.

"No—only you. When people go to all that trouble to keep a marriage secret there's sometimes a reason. Maybe Mrs. Holden wasn't an official widow, or maybe . . . Anyway, I'd rather have things go on exactly as usual while

I see what I can find out. Just don't look surprised at any errands I may invent, will you?"

Joanna was a remarkably good dissembler. It was in a tone of mild annoyance that she remembered, at dinner that night, a baby shower for Sue Wallace the following evening. "Remember the girl I was telling you about, Kate?" There was nothing but open inquiry in her gaze. "Damn—that means staying the night if I don't want to tackle that drive after dark, but I don't suppose I can get out of it now."

Gerald said reflectively, "Even savages don't have showers," and Georgia asked idly what Joanna was bringing.

"Fitted crib sheets," said Joanna, just promptly enough. "I thought she'd be deluged with those little Philippine dresses."

She left the next afternoon, presumably for Vermont. Gerald, cheerfully unaware of his disinherited status, insisted on taking Georgia and Kate to dinner. They were having a liqueur when the corner of Kate's eye saw Carpenter approaching between the tables.

Why should she flinch inwardly, and preoccupy herself with the stem of her tiny glass when his voice said casually above her, "Family outing?"

"The cat's away," explained Gerald amiably, and Kate knew without looking up that there would be a faint stern crease between Georgia's perfect eyebrows. "Join us?"

"Thanks, but we're on our way," said Carpenter, and added vaguely that he'd see them soon. Kate raised her cool glance at the end and then dropped it before she could see who "we" were; it was not as if she cared.

In the morning, there was another of the dreaded envelopes from Bridgeport.

Destroy it unopened? The mailing time on the postmark told Kate it could not be in answer to her own letter and money; besides, those sickening loops and curls meant only one thing. But suppose it were a fresh line of attack, something she had to know about to defend herself against?

It was another clipping: "Hornet Causes Fatality," and under that, "Fresno, Calif.—An eleven-year-old boy's prank took the lives of his mother and sister yesterday when Frank Medwick, annoyed at the demands of Ann Medwick, 14, for candy, captured a hornet in the family car and offered it to her in a candy wrapper. The girl's screams caused Mrs. Marie Medwick to lose control of the car, and an oncoming truck—"

Kate stopped reading there, but not before she heard the crinkle of paper, the furious rattle of the released hornet, the boy's innocent laugh before the shriller sounds of tragedy.

How could Mrs. Maynard, how could anyone, be so brutal?

In her apartment, Kate wrote with fierce tumbling haste: "Dear Mr. Maynard—As I've already written, I sympathize fully with your wife's condition, but I will not be subjected to any more of the enclosed. I ought to let you know that I will destroy any further communication such as this unopened. Katherine Barlow."

She placed the envelope with its clipping inside her own and then, because this was too urgent to wait, went out to her car. Although the windows were tightly closed, she carried out her usual wasp inspection before starting the engine, with particular care to sunny, cunning places like the top side of the sun-shield, the faint slope of the padded dashboard, the space just under the rear window. She shut her mind, as she drove to the nearest collection box, to the thought of the hornet loose in Mrs. Medwick's car.

It seemed to take an eternity to get to her goal and back, but then, she discovered, she had been driving at a damp, tense fifteen miles an hour.

With the letter sent, the ultimatum laid down, she had a queer sense of timelessness. She typed Carpenter's copy until her fingers began to make mistakes in rebellion, but she had to admire it: in this telling, Virgil Beal Scott seemed to rank with John Paul Jones and Thomas Alva Edison. Joanna, back from her investigating trip to Vermont, had only a mute shake of the head which Kate hardly noticed.

The Maynards had already received the money and the letter in which she explained her own financial circumstances, and she could only guess at their reaction to that— acceptance, indignation, a regret that they had not brought suit at once? By tomorrow they would have a second note, refusing to tolerate a campaign of terror. Unfortunately this brought a clearer image, of Mrs. Maynard's pale red-rimmed eyes flashing in her knifelike face, her voice rising hysterically, Barney coming in fear to watch and listen . . .

In spite of the drowsy nausea she knew it would bring, Kate took a sleeping pill that night and the next, and had her tranquilizer prescription refilled. She was now frightened almost as much by sight as by sound; a wind-blown burr lying harmlessly on her doorstep, or a tiny shred of dark paper, sent her shying back with a sprinkle of physical fear through her chest.

In one of the unreal sleeping-pill interludes, she imagined someone muffled and huge-headed walking slowly along the line of bushes at the back of the property, carrying a shielded light. But when she asked casually about the bee-veil the next morning, Gerald said, "Oh, that went back to Carpenter, it belongs to his aunt," and gave a little ripple of aversion. "She used to keep bees, if you can imagine such a thing. How fond can one be of honey?"

On the third day after her own frantically written note, Kate got a reply from Maynard. Her gaze skipped past the opening civilities, and there, burned like fire into the cheap paper, were the words she had invited upon her own head.

"Sue . . ."

". . . witness."

X

WITNESS.

For a twisted second it was almost like a word in a love letter, so catching the breath and dizzying the gaze that any further reading must be anticlimax. Briefly, Kate saw nothing at all, and then the typed lines came into vision again.

Maynard thanked her for the money, somewhat briskly, and went on to say that he had just installed his wife in a private nursing home. "It is expensive but the other ones are full of old sick people and the doctor says that would be the worst thing for her condition." He and Barney had found a clean quiet room not far from the nursing home and it was nice to be away from his brother-in-law's.

"My bro-in-law—" how that began to grate "—kept saying we should sue, as Barney looks very Queer to him and especialley as we have this witness who saw the whole thing."

Desperation pressed so tightly against Kate's temples that it was like having her head caught in a window. No acknowledgement of her explanation that her own financial help could go no farther, no mention of her note about the vicious clippings. Instead, a bewildering reference to "the whole thing"—as though she had concealed some shameful piece of information—and something that was not quite a threat.

". . . we have this witness": it was very much in the present tense. But the road had been completely empty; Kate remembered the impact of her voice on the dappled silence. Someone looking out a window, then, one of the Maynards' neighbors?

Kate knew what was called for, at least in theory. A cool letter back, stating that Barney had shot without warning through an open gate into the path of her car, that the hedge rendered the gate invisible to an approaching driver, and that she had already and of her own volition provided all the financial assistance of which she was capable. In effect: go ahead and sue.

But suppose they did?

Appearances were hopelessly against her. Even if a jury would not automatically side with the trouble-ridden parents of a frightened and stammering child, a strong suggestion could and undoubtedly would be made that she and not Robert had been at the wheel in that fatal crash in Arizona. They had both been flung clear; there was only her word for it that Robert had been driving. Certainly it would be made to seem a singular coincidence that she had been involved in two accidents only eleven months apart.

On top of that, she remembered with a flesh flicker of alarm that she had held out her driver's license to Maynard as identification. Had he noticed the expiration date? He had certainly read it before handing it back. Who would believe that it was at his insistence she hadn't reported the accident? Wouldn't the volunteered thousand dollars, in this light, have all the air of a bribe?

. . . And here it came again, the flashing dampness, the terrifying unrelatedness to physical things around her. A lamp seemed to bow very delicately toward her, and Kate moved her gaze slowly and carefully away and saw the rug slide with it. She told her body savagely that it was not going to topple from the couch, that this was only the trickery of nerves and everything would be normal in a minute.

It was more than a minute—and suppose it should happen to her on a witness stand? She would explain, in vain, that it never occurred when her attention was physically occupied, as in driving, and that she had been free of it for months before the accident. She could hear the skeptical, "Oh, indeed? How fortunate, Mrs. Barlow."

Gerald would be worse than no witness at all. He would be staunchly against tricycles, gates, hedges, and, if it seemed necessary, four-year-old boys.

Kate would have to find the Maynards' witness.

She had to steel herself to leave the apartment, in spite of her new urgency. The morning was hot and still, and wasps lingered lazily through it like goldfish in a bowl. Other, unnoticing people might not see them, but Kate did. They touched lightly on the windowsills, crawled, spiralled off as though remembering an errand somewhere, and came back. Around the lilac—in search of some long-fallen blossom?—hovered a large yellow-jacket, pointed body arced and ready.

They would have no interest in perfumeless Kate . . . would they? Yes, if she ran on this syrupy morning. Twice she put out a hand to the screen door, thinking that her determination might wrap her like a cloak, and twice she drew it back. Before her third and successful try she put on a white cardigan over her thin bare-armed dress; she would stifle in it, but it gave her a false feeling of protection. Or not quite false: an outer garment could always be wriggled out of with infinite delicacy, shed, fled from.

Except for her visits to the Maynards since the day of the accident, Kate had avoided Maple Avenue although it meant going miles out of her way. Now she approached it with a sick acceleration of the heart; it looked all the more dangerous for its cunningly innocent pattern of leaves and sunlight. Somewhere inside the pattern was the witness who had told the Maynards—what?

Slowly, now; she would have to measure the angles of view very carefully. The houses on either side of the Maynards' could not be discounted, in spite of the screening hedge and maple branches, because someone might have been standing at an upstairs window. But the houses across the street seemed much more likely, and there were only three of them in the possible line of vision. Kate turned her car into the driveway of the first.

Like the others, it was small, standardized, vaguely Dutch Colonial; an attempt at departure had been made in brightly staring blue shutters and an ornamental screen door. There was a playpen in the little front yard, and toys and a blanket gave it a just-vacated look in spite of the silence about the place. Kate had to battle an impulse to back out again and drive safely away, because what, in essence, must she say to a perfect stranger? "Did you happen to see me hit the Maynard boy a few weeks ago?"

It had to be done, unless she were to live under a shapeless threat that might even now be gathering form and purpose. Even if the witness thought her deliberately negligent he would lead her to the Maynards, and surely if they discussed the whole thing face to face instead of through the mails—

The door opened without warning on a pretty blonde girl with a young baby cradled against her shoulder. Kate had read the name on the mailbox, and she said what was to become a formula: "Mrs. Talley? I'm Katherine Barlow—you don't know me, but I wonder if I could talk to you for a few minutes? It's quite important to me."

Mrs. Talley looked oddly hesitant, but at last she stepped back and allowed Kate to enter a tiny hall. She said with firmness, "If you'll wait here for just a minute, I'll put the baby down," and vanished up the stairs. Kate's heart beat harder, because if she were not the witness, why had the girl given her that peculiar look, a combination of hostility and interest?

Footsteps echoed faintly above, there was a wheeling sound of casters. Kate, scrupulously avoiding so much as a glance into what was visible of the living room, gazed instead at a small oval mirror and saw herself with an actual shock.

No wonder the girl had stared. She was wearing a sundress on this roasting day, and the baby a diaper and

talcum powder—and here was Kate muffled to the throat
and wrists in a sweater. As a result, her face was damp
and brilliantly flushed, and with the new accentuation of
eyelids and cheekbones she looked like someone in delir-
ium—or, less kindly, an escaped mental patient. She opened
her bag with a vague notion of effecting repairs, so that
when the blonde girl came running down the stairs she had
all the air of just having stolen something.

"It's so hot," said Kate, producing a handkerchief, and
the empty words brought forth instantly the answer she
wanted. Mrs. Talley, apparently relieved at so humdrum a
remark from such an unstrung-looking creature, said that
it certainly was hot, and the baby felt it all the more because she had just brought him back from Maine, where
they had stayed with her family for two months.

"I'm afraid the house is a mess," she said, glancing deprecatingly about the spotless floors and shining windows.
"My husband got so lonesome after the first couple of
days that he went to stay at his sister's . . . what did you
say I could help you about?"

Nothing, now, but Kate had to produce an answer of
some kind. "Well, it—was just something about the Maynards, the people across the street, but as you weren't
here . . ."

"We didn't know them at all anyway," said Mrs. Talley
with finality, and put a hand on the doorknob.

Upstairs, as though to underline the gesture, the baby
began a fretful whimpering. Kate thanked the blonde girl
and left, taking away with her a strong impression of dis-
approval—of the Maynards, or of prying strangers?

The next mailbox said Henderson. Miss Henderson, who
lived alone, was a great tall morose woman who pounced
upon Kate as a break in the day's monotony. When Kate
asked about the Maynards her eyes grew shrewd. "You
wouldn't be trying to collect a bill? I hear they owed all
over town."

Then, at Kate's shake of the head, "I wouldn't know,
myself. I'd see him outside now and again—of course, up

until last week I didn't get home until six, I've been working at the library since Mrs. Moffatt went on maternity leave in June . . ."

Briefly, Kate stopped listening. This was not the Maynards' witness, because with a job she would not have been home at the time of the accident.

"—Mrs. Maynard was sick," said Miss Henderson's re-entering voice. "Middle-ear trouble, her husband told me once, but she didn't look blood-pressurey to me, a little bit of a thing like that."

Her gaze was inquiring, but Kate could not cope with this swift diagnosis. She said instead, "They had a little boy, didn't they?"

"Oh, and a nice-mannered child, yes ma'am and no ma'am, very anxious to please," said Miss Henderson approvingly. "I wonder where they went, poor things? And will you look at that?"

It happened with bewildering speed. At the indignant change in Miss Henderson's voice Kate turned her head obediently toward the small window above and behind her left shoulder, and felt her chest explode with panic at the wasps—three? four?—crawling soundlessly there. She took a violent step backward and to her right, sending a table crashing, and in the same instant Miss Henderson produced a large handkerchief and took a vengeful swipe at the window. One wasp shot past Kate's face; another, stunned, fell on her sweatered shoulder. With her gasp of terror sounding louder than a scream in the little hallway, she swept blindly at the place, felt the brief touch of the wasp, at once hard and feathery against her finger, and collided cruelly with the newel post.

Time escaped her trickily there. Even with her head turned rigidly away she knew that Miss Henderson, breathing hard, was battling victoriously with the wasps, and that presently the fallen table was being set back on its legs, but she had no idea of how long it took.

"Well, I must say—!" began Miss Henderson in a tone of astonished anger, and looked at Kate and broke off. "I'll

89

get you a glass of water," she said, and went hastily away.

Kate drank the cold water gratefully, and forced her breath to come slowly against the frightening pain in her chest. To Miss Henderson, who was now watching her with keen interest, she said laboredly, "I'm sorry. I don't—know what—came over me."

"Maybe you're allergic to wasps. I have a sister-in-law like that, and when she got stung once they gave her a tetanus shot, and she reacted so badly they had to give her strychnine, and that," said Miss Henderson with faint relish, "nearly finished her off." She glanced up at the window. "There must be a nest under the eaves somewhere."

And one of the inhabitants had seen Kate, and signalled to the others—for just a second, she pressed her hands fiercely against her face. Then she said shakily, taking a step toward the door, "Well, I'm sorry. And I hope I haven't ruined your table."

"Oh, that old thing," said Miss Henderson disparagingly. "Do you think you ought to go out just yet?"

Kate said that she would be perfectly all right, but at the door she paused. Another walk through treacherous sunlight, another wait under possibly wasp-laden eaves—without much hope, she asked Miss Henderson about the people who lived next door.

There was nothing that Miss Henderson would not now have done to oblige this interesting creature who went berserk in hallways at the sight of a wasp. "The Clifts. They're good friends of mine—we play canasta almost every night —but you wouldn't find them home because they both work."

And that was why Maple Avenue had been so quiet that first day; all of these houses had been empty and eyeless. Kate was still badly shaken, and in her sweltering car she smoked a cigarette with a hand that felt boneless and unsteady before she had strength and accuracy enough to make the last of her inquiries. If she drove away now, she would never have the courage to come back. And the witness was here, had to be here, in one of the houses that flanked the Maynards'.

But, at the end of half an hour, the witness was not. At the first house, a woman with a face like a dinosaur's and a menacing headful of curlers told Kate flatly that she didn't know anything about the Maynards. Nor did she care, obviously. Most of her attention was concentrated on a loud soap opera emanating from another room, so that Kate's few questions fell weakly down among furious accusations, sobbing denials, and significant burst of organ music.

"Today is Yours is on next," said the woman, and closed the door conclusively in Kate's face.

The house on the other side of the Maynards' bore a sun-yellowed sign in one front window: "Alterations. Phone G14-8793 week-ends or after 5:30 P.M." There was, as Kate had expected, no response to her ring.

Was it possible that the Maynards had warned their witness to silence—blonde young Mrs. Talley, the somehow wistful Miss Henderson, or the dinosaur woman in curlers? None of them had rung false.

But neither had Maynard's ". . . we have this witness."

The purr of a very soft motor brought Kate's head around. The dressmaker's car returning after all? No. Mr. Symmes' long black Cadillac, vanishing into the sun-and-shadowed distance.

XI

DINNER was unusually quiet. Even through her own pre-occupation, Kate noticed a rare depth of gloom in Gerald, and presently she found out why: having lost a large contract to a competing firm, Mr. Symmes had promptly halved all vacations wherever he had the power to do so.

Gerald and Joanna had had the offer of a friend's cottage in Provincetown; now, all of the packing and driving and provision-buying would not be worth while. Kate risked a lightning glance at Joanna's face, and to her surprise found it only thoughtful.

"You know," said Joanna, lashes down as she toyed with a leaf of salad, "I think if he were asked nicely he might change his mind."

"Ha," said Gerald spiritlessly.

"He certainly might," said Georgia with unusual sharpness. "He might cut out your vacation altogether."

"It's the kind of thing that would occur to him," admitted Gerald.

"No, I really think that if I explained things to him he might give in," said Joanna serenely, and for just a second her face wore a look that Kate, even knowing what she knew, found inexpressibly shocking: it had the mocking, almost dreamy innocence of a child's who really plans to burn a bound playmate at the stake.

So she had managed to find out something about the secret Symmes-Holden marriage to use as a weapon—which was hardly Kate's affair, or was it? After her glimpse of the Symmes car on Maple Avenue, she had argued

92

fruitlessly with herself all the way home. Maple Avenue was a public thoroughfare, and the Symmes' had every right to use it; attaching any significance to their presence there, on just that day, would be as ridiculous as if they were to find it sinister when she drove past the large ugly house on King's Court Road.

Besides, Maple Avenue had been empty on the afternoon that mattered. Or as far as Kate knew; what about the time when she was in the Maynards' house? Her car had been parked in front, with a crushed tricycle under the near wheel and Gerald in the passenger seat for all the world to see. And to anyone who knew Gerald it was perfectly conceivable that, wrapped in his anxiety, he had not seen his father's car go by.

But that did not constitute being a witness, and what possible motive could Mr. Symmes have for allying himself with the Maynards? Except that you did not really have to examine motives where such random malice was concerned.

Joanna's odd new blandness—because she was certainly very pleased about something—altered the situation a little. If Mr. Symmes had discovered any trace of her probing into his marriage, he would arm himself with any weapon at hand. Kate did not know to what, if any extent a passenger was culpable in not reporting an accident, particularly if it should develop into a lawsuit; she did know enough about Mr. Symmes to be sure that he would do what he could.

"Kate, I thought you like crab-meat salad," said Joanna's reproachful voice, "and just look at your plate."

Everybody looked, and what had formerly been a cool pale-pink distribution over lettuce now appeared such a mountain to Kate that she picked up her fork obediently. She had reckoned without her stomach, so knotted with tension that it might have had ten full dinners; she got a morsel down, barely.

"Too hot to eat, really," said Gerald, and then glanced abashedly at his own empty plate.

"You must eat, Kate," said Georgia in her soft practical voice. "Really, I don't understand you. Even when—"

She stopped there, or her voice did; the silence stated it ringingly: "Even when Robert was killed it didn't affect you like this."

("Robert was an idol, and nothing less . . .")

Kate did not attempt a defense, even in her own despairing mind. She inspected her crab meat steadily, realized that her fingers were curving the hair over her temple in their old bad habit, and locked her hands in her lap.

Glances must have been exchanged then, because conversation broke out simultaneously on three sides.

"Did you—"

"I saw Mrs.—"

"The television man—"

Kate smiled wryly. "Thank you," she said. "Is everybody ready for coffee?"

She and Joanna did the dishes. Georgia had departed for the living room and television, and Gerald sat moodily at the kitchen table with a second cup of coffee. Kate wondered fleetingly if he were as unaware of his changed situation as Joanna thought; his long-lashed olive eyes looked very somber indeed. Joanna seemed not to notice; her own profile was calm and secret.

One of Georgia's few stiffnesses was a kitchen left immaculate for morning—steel sink wiped dry, ashtrays polished to a glitter, telephone and electric clock in precise alignment. Kate was straightening the pad beside the telephone when she saw the note.

Mrs. Nairn, the once-a-week cleaning-woman, had been at the house that day; because there was her speedy black scrawl and the "Mrs. Kate" with which she separated one Mrs. Barlow from the other. "A man called," said the message. "Will call back."

Maynard.

It was partly a lightning recognition in Kate's brain, partly the sensible fact that Carpenter, the only other man

man who might have called, would never have acted so anonymously. It seemed bitterly ironic that while she had been progressing futilely up and down Maple Avenue, Maynard had been in search of her.

Why? Because they had decided to sue?

Kate said her good-nights a little coolly; the fact that they must all have seen the message, and none of them had mentioned it to her, made her stiff. A man, they would think; well, that would explain her new absences from the apartment, her strange behavior.

When would Maynard call again?

In the apartment she closed the door behind her; although the screen door had a hook on the inside, and there was a slight stir of coolness in the lilac, she felt uneasy about being exposed to the night. Until now she had regarded the hours of darkness as the safest, when wasps and bees were in their nests, but she did not examine the illogicality of this.

What to do in the immediate space of time ahead? Certainly not stare tensely at the phone, wondering if Maynard were even now trying to reach her, because in that case it would never ring. Kate took a fast shower, changed into her coolest robe, found herself gazing long and blankly at things like the faucets, her shower cap, the toe of her slipper. She saw nothing of any of them, just as she had not seen her own thin distraught reflection.

Whatever Maynard had to say to her, it was unthinkable that she should pay again, even if her funds were bottomless. It had been shock and compassion the first time, a sense of responsibility the second time. This time it would be submitting to blackmail.

If the Maynards had decided to bring suit, and it was hard to think of any other reason for the telephone call, they would move swiftly in the face of Kate's rebellion. She would have to find a lawyer at once, and she would also have to find money. She had never been involved in a lawsuit but she knew that it was an expensive process, particularly if you lost—and it was very probable indeed that she would lose.

The alternative was living in thrall to the Maynards, waiting in dread for another of the circuitous, archaically capitalled demands, becoming their creature until it seemed a natural part of her existence.

The phone rang.

Kate forced herself not to snatch up the receiver, because the call might not be for her at all. After a heart-beating pause it rang again, and she let it ring twice more, as though she were unafraid, before she picked up the receiver and said very crisply, "Hello?"

"You sound a trifle warlike," said Carpenter's voice mild-ly in her ear. "Anything the matter?"

"Oh . . . no." Kate clenched her fingers around the receiver, because he was tying up the line, sending out a busy signal to Bridgeport. "I hope the manuscript's all right?"

"You've done everything but illuminate it. The only thing," said Carpenter, sounding at once amused and apologetic, "is—you know the black bear cub Scott is supposed to have tamed only we know better?"

"Barnum, you mean."

"Yes, but he's turned into Barney in the last forty pages. Have I a rival in—I can't call them your affections, can I?" inquired Carpenter distantly.

He said something else, but Kate didn't hear it; for a second or two her throat ached and almost filled with despair. She had thought work her salvation, and had gone at it so eagerly, and even in this impersonal area her disintegrating nerves had trapped her. She could not trust herself at all now; indeed, what other unreliable thing might she have done in the past few days?

The silence stretched out. Kate said stiffly into it, "I'm sorry, I don't know what I could have been thinking of. If you'll be home tomorrow morning I'll pick—"

"Oh, I've fixed it," said Carpenter cheerfully.

Ask him about a lawyer now? With his unsurpriseable

quality he would probably give her the name of one, without questions. Kate drew breath, and heard over the wire a distant sound of chimes. "Somebody at the door," said Carpenter rapidly. "Good-night, Kate. Take care."

Oh, dear, yes. Watch what she said, and above all what she wrote—on checks, for instance. Wearily, appalled at this new aspect of herself, Kate stayed up until eleven o'clock, but Maynard did not telephone. When she did go to bed it was only to get up again, twice: had she really put out that last cigarette, and was the front door actually locked? And her car windows. If they weren't rolled up, the warmth of the early sun on metal and glass would attract the first spiralling wasp . . .

She had to force herself to go out into the dark; it was as though somewhere in it disaster waited for her quietly and contentedly. But it was only a matter of damp unshaven grass, a few curls of doorway light in the lilac, a night bird that sounded—such was the state of her nerves —like someone sneezing.

Her car windows were rolled up after all, but the distance between the driveway and the golden apartment door seemed to have lengthened slyly. Kate ran through it like a moving target, wrenched at the screen, and managed to kick herself violently in the ankle while pulling it shut before moths could get in. She was just in time; there was a swift stutter of wings against the mesh, and the glimpse of a tiny alert face, before she slammed the inner door and snapped off the light.

In the morning, she saw the newspaper picture that changed everything.

It came about indirectly as a result of Joanna's sudden suggestion that they go to the beach. "You like to swim, Kate, and it would do you good to get away for an hour or so."

When Maynard might call? "Gray Beach is full of jellyfish," said Kate evasively.

"But Ham's Point in Bridgeport isn't, or Spiller's Beach."

Kate felt her nerves tightening under the well-meant persistence. "They'd be jammed."

"The water wouldn't be," pointed out Georgia, idle but practical. "Most people who go to beaches don't know how to swim."

Which was true—but then Gerald, who escaped on Saturdays from the tyranny of the plant, came to Kate's rescue. "I'm not so sure of that. Did you see the spread in last night's *Sentinel?*"

Georgia never read an evening paper because it spoiled the television news; Kate seldom went beyond the front page and foreign coverage; Joanna confined herself to hooting at the editorials and making fun of the society page. Gerald ambled off and presently returned with a newspaper which, opened wide, engulfed a good part of the table. "Look at that," he said. "They may not be able to swim, but they can certainly clutter up the water."

Everybody looked, automatically. It was the kind of double-spread run by city papers in the summer doldrums. Under the caption "Record-Breaking Heat Draws Crowds to Local Beaches" were all the regulation pictures: the thronged umbrella-starred sands, the water packed with humanity like sardines on end, the pretty high-school girls with a striped ball, the absorbed baby in the process of losing its diminutive trunks.

In all of them, as intended, the crowd background was there. Kate gazed, and felt her heart check.

She wasn't sure until nearly three hours later, in a small "Enlargements while you wait" photo studio in Bridgeport. She had already visited the offices of the *Sentinel,* and, with a number of winning lies about the nearly naked baby's striking resemblance to her own little niece, been able to buy a print of the photograph she wanted.

"Sure is a cute little tyke," said the clerk falsely, handing Kate a glossy enlargement.

"Yes, isn't she?" Kate was blind to everything but the sharpened background.

Barney wasn't there, but Maynard was, his bull's head thrown back in an almost audible shout of laughter. Beside him was Mrs. Maynard—Mrs. Maynard of the grief-pinched face and reddened eyes and trembling hands—in less of a bathing suit than would have been allowed on most beaches, with her pony-tailed profile turned roguishly toward the man whose arm was draped familiarly about her shoulders. He wore a handkerchief knotted grotesquely about his head, and one hand cradled a can of beer against his luridly tattooed chest.

Dr. Sanders. Or the man who had said he was Dr. Sanders.

XII

IT was a rebellion of anger that got Kate home. She had taken the bus to Bridgeport, not trusting herself to drive that far in traffic, and she found that she had just missed a bus and had to wait a further twenty minutes. People stared at her openly, and probably, with what she had just learned, she was something to stare at. She did not even mind the indicating elbows, the elaborately trained-back gazes that came to focus curiously on her face.

She had to remind herself that she still did not know about Barney—but she knew other things. That Mrs. Maynard, as revealed in the leftovers of a Bikini, was certainly not wasting away of "Melancollia" in a nursing home; that the solemn J. Maynard of the letters had his moments of vast amusement; that the brusque Dr. Sanders ("I'd rather see the boy alone, if you don't mind, Mrs. Maynard") was certainly more friend than doctor.

How easy to remove an "M.D." symbol from a car in a hospital parking lot, if you really wanted one, and how easy to rattle off phrases. Medical terms were so eagerly assimilated by laymen that they could almost anticipate doctors; you heard the most random reference to "post-operative shock" and "massive collapse."

For this she had lain awake identifying herself with another nerve-stricken women; for this she had pictured Maynard awkwardly ministering to his wife and small son—Maynard, roaring laughing, with another man's arm close about his wife's coquettishly turned shoulders.

There was a wasp beating dryly against the rear win-

100

dow of the bus, so that although there were seats Kate
stood at the front, clutching a pole and ready to flee at the
first stop if it were necessary. The driver watched her
whitened, sharpened face uneasily for a time in his mirror;
when he said, "There's seats in back, lady," she only answered mechanically, "Thank you, but I'd rather stand.
I've been sitting for quite a while."

. . . Like a duck. How often did it happen, all over
the country? Kate knew of a woman, a friend of a friend's,
who had stumbled on an uneven crack in the town pavement and collected five thousand dollars for a broken foot.
The woman had said later, complacently, that she had
been wearing new sandals and would have tripped, my
dear, on the absolute level.

A man at the back of the bus swept his newspaper at
the wasp and it soared forward, hitting the roof, coming
seekingly down again. When the doors opened, Kate flew
down the steps although it left her nearly a mile to walk
in the scalding heat.

They had done this to her, too. The horror of wasps
and bees and anything that flew had sprung full-fledged
out of her encounter with Barney. If she could prove that
as false as everything else connected with the Maynards,
she knew it suddenly and quite clearly, the horror would
be exorcised.

She was faint when she reached the apartment; she
had, she realized, eaten no lunch. She approached the
door warily, knowing the lure of sun-warmed wood, and
presently two shadows drifted lazily on the clapboards,
reeling up and down as though controlled by rhythmic,
invisible strings. What was it that made them speed by
like tracer bullets at other times, and why did they find
Kate's apartment more attractive than the house? She di-
rected her mind forcibly away from that, because there lay
complete disintegration.

The back of the apartment was in shadow, and she let
herself in the door there and stood listening a moment
with the sense that had grown expert, that could filter the

close jerky sound of wasp out of all the surrounding country sounds. Then she stepped tiredly out of her sandals,
tossed her bag and gloves at a chair and collapsed on the
couch, head back and eyelids down. She knew what she
would have to do, but not yet, not for a few minutes . . .

She didn't sleep, although she ached all over with strain
and fatigue; the newly crystallized necessity of seeing Barney Maynard for herself pricked at her like a needle.
Presently she got up and went into the bathroom to wash
a face whose reflection frightened her: except for a ring
of white about the mouth, it was an angry scarlet. A cold
dripping cloth held repeatedly against her cheeks and
forehead helped a little, and half an hour later, reduced
to a flushed pink, she crossed the shadowed lawn to the
house.

Because it was not the official end of her nap, Georgia's voice sounded pettish from behind her bedroom
door. "Who is it?"

"Kate. I'm sorry to bother you, but I'd like to talk to
you."

"Oh . . . just a minute." There was a faint exasperated
creak of released bedsprings, the jostle of moving fabric,
and then a cautious interval of silence, as though Georgia
were taking off her eye pads and giving herself a swift
defensive examination in the mirror. Kate stared steadily at
her sandalled toes, and the door opened.

Georgia's room was big and pretty, a cool-headed combination of business and pleasure. The bed had a bill-
owy flowered flounce, but across from it stood a desk with
a straight chair before it. There was a dressing table
crowded with bottles and jars and tubes; beside it on a
table was an office file.

Georgia straightened the coverlet with one of her competent gestures. "Sit down, Kate, you look dreadfully hot."
She sat down herself, gaze frankly examining, hands automatically brushing up wisps of hair at the nape of her
neck. "You haven't some foolish notion about the apartment again?"

"No. I wondered if you were still interested in buying land."

Georgia's hands halted and then came slowly down. "Robert's land?"

"Well, mine now," said Kate, smiling a little stiffly. She felt ridiculously nervous. "I've realized that I can't live this way indefinitely, even if I weren't underfoot all the time, and I thought that with capital—I might invest . . ."

The nonsense came babbling out of its own accord. It might not have, a moment before; Kate hadn't planned ahead. But if she told Georgia the truth at this juncture, mightn't there be, as well as the solemn Barlow censure of her own weakness and folly, a very real anger at this disposal of "Robert's" money, and a determination to put a stop to it? They would firmly disown the Maynards, root and branch, and they were three against Kate's sick, necessitous one. And being disciples of strength—except Gerald, who would be borne helplessly along with them—they would never understand or admit Kate's motive in finding and talking to Barney Maynard.

A door slammed in the driveway; Joanna was back. Georgia said distressedly, "I think you're making a great mistake, Kate. That land has already appreciated, and it might go a lot higher. I'm quite sure that Robert intended you to keep it."

A nerve leaped in Kate's temple. "Yes, I know. On the other hand," she stood up, in a sudden panic that the room might begin to tilt and slip around her, "he did leave me executor. If you aren't interested, I imagine there are—"

"Oh, I'm interested," said Georgia in a changed voice. Her blue eyes had lost their softness, and a forgotten smear of the cream she had removed gave her face a surprising gloss and definition. She left her chair and crossed to the desk, pulling down the flap with an unusual roughness. "I'm just—surprised, I suppose, that you don't trust me, Kate. If you needed money, it could have been found somehow without—"

Neither of them had heard the telephone ring down-stairs; both of them heard the crisp summons of Joanna's voice. "Mother? Can you talk to the Welfare Committee?"

Georgia opened the bedroom door. "Tell them—" she called, and then glanced distractedly back at Kate. "Wait," she said, and vanished.

I will walk around very quietly, Kate promised her increasingly frightened body, and look only at small close things. And she did. Damp and unsteady, she kept her control by staying in slow and careful motion and gazing with desperate attention at objects and surfaces within her immediate focus; any long glance, through a window, would separate her from her balance instantly.

She felt eerily quiet within, as though her heart had stopped beating and it would take only seconds for the rest of her to discover it. One hand went independently to her chest, and the suddenness of the movement, or the attendant fear, gave her a sensation of staggering. She put her other hand out hard to the desk flap Georgia had lowered, and the desk rocked a little with a papery chatter of spilled envelopes.

Kate stared fiercely at the flowered flouncing of the bed; she would not fall in a sick crumple on Georgia's floor; this was only nerves, the doctor had said so. Gradually the room sharpened and hardened around her, her heart seemed to be going about its usual business, she was able to take her leaning hand from the desk flap.

. . . And push the toppled wedge of envelopes back into the proper pigeonhole, if only because the desk now had a look of having been ransacked. But there must have been something at the back of the space, because under the lifting pressures of her fingers the envelopes flew resistantly apart, three of them skidding from flap to floor.

It was odd, or perhaps it wasn't, how your own name identified itself leapingly even in an almost unseeing glance. The seconds ticked by while Kate stood rootedly still, holding two windowed envelopes addressed to her from the Bureau of Motor Vehicles. From the postmarks and the printing visible through the slot, they were her application for renewal of her driver's license and her license itself.

Georgia came back in a swish of housecoat folds, wearing a pleasedly dedicated air. "I know you make fun of committees, Kate, but I've always thought that if you got out more, and saw people whose troubles are— What's the matter?"

"Nothing. I'm just glad to have found my driver's license—by accident," Kate said, scrupulously calm. "I leaned against your desk and some things fell out. It's quite a relief to have it at last."

An odd expression, too swift for analysis, flashed across Georgia's face. Then she was saying in a shocked voice, "You don't really mean that I was so stupid as to—" She inspected the envelopes in Kate's hand, ruefully. "Yes, apparently, I was. Kate, I'm terribly sorry. I suppose these came in with a flock of bills and I just put them all away together. How lucky that you weren't stopped!"

"Yes." And how meticulous Georgia always was about bills; her rare moments of open irritation usually sprang from any negligence in that quarter.

"Well, all's well that ends well," said Georgia, falsely sunny, "and I promise to be more careful. Now, are you absolutely sure about the land. . . ?"

But her mind was clearly not on the land, nor was Kate's. It took half an hour of conscious politeness, and a meticulous call to the real estate broker Robert had dealt with, to establish a fair price for the acreage. At the end of that time, Kate was assured of five thousand dollars within the next two or three days; she did not look beyond that to the fact that she had used up most of her last resource.

When Georgia said simply at her bedroom door, "I'm sorry about this, very," Kate could only look silently down at her hands. Georgia meant that she was sorry about the land; she seemed to have dismissed very lightly the onus of having retained someone else's driver's license. Because while it was possible that one envelope from the Motor Vehicles Bureau might have wandered mistakenly into the possession of the elder Mrs. Barlow, it was hardly conceivable that two should have.

Joanna was halfway out the front door when Kate got downstairs; she said airily over her shoulder, "Look who's here," and slipped through, a blade of navy-and-white silk stripes against the ripening afternoon light. Anyone driving by, thought Kate removedly, watching her approach Mr. Symmes on the lawn with every appearance of cordiality, would gather an impression of ease and pleasure: there was the long gleaming car in the drive, the wide clipped law, the handsome house behind it. How many existences were tooth and claw like this, how many savageries lingered behind surface gestures, like Joanna's solicitous arm through her father-in-law's as they walked toward the apartment?

There were unmistakable signs of alien occupancy there, but Joanna would no longer care; she was very much in the driver's seat. Kate felt a small surprising tug of sympathy for Mr. Symmes as she dropped down on the end of the couch to wait. Joanna had evidently confided in her mother at last, because the house was completely silent; there was to be, today, no fluster over butter knives.

The minutes went by, the apartment door slantingly visible across the lawn remained closed, the two envelopes began to wilt under the tense pressure of Kate's fingers. Georgia had thought her unfit to drive, and had, quite successfully, curtailed her driving activities—but why had she thought so before the accident, when the application for renewal had come? Had Kate shown signs of instability even then, when she had believed so innocently that her nerves were healed?

Her face burned all over again at an imaginary discussion, involving Carpenter. Georgia and Joanna would have told him decidedly that Kate was not recovering as she should, that perhaps the therapy of work, the facing up to responsibility again, would do what time and cossetting had not. She was a good typist, would he give her a chance?

Kate stood up, because the apartment door had opened. Mr. Symmes came out, followed by Joanna, and walked directly to his car; there seemed to be no parting amenities. Joanna waved as he left, but it seemed the kind of appreciative salute the cat might have given the canary feathers.

Kate said automatically, "Did you arrange things?" and Joanna gave her a cool imperturbable look. "He really isn't so terribly unreasonable when you get him alone. Gerald does rub him the wrong way sometimes, and I knew the situation only needed explaining."

"How nice anyway," said Kate to the clear rebuff, and crossed the lawn to the apartment. It might have been resentment that made her reclaim the place instantly as her own, moving back a chair that had been moved forward, emptying Joanna's half-smoked cigarettes and Mr. Symmes' frayed cigar end from the ashtrays, gathering up her pocketbook and gloves from the drawer where Joanna had placed them. It was certainly imagination that made her think the apartment altered somehow.

A lawyer was far more important now than any speculation about her driver's license; if possible, she must make her move before the Maynards did. The yellow pages of the telephone book listed a number of lawyers. Kate knew from Joanna that Snaith and Snaith handled mainly estates, and she had heard that Cupples, Robertson and Kuhn were especially sought out for divorce. How to find a lawyer who would help her in the matter of a child she had—as a driver with a lapsed license—injured to an unknown extent?

Carpenter would know; it was the kind of information with which he acquainted himself in an interested but impersonal way. Kate picked up the phone and dialled his number, and replaced the receiver after a number of unavailing rings. He was out—or perhaps he was merely outdoors, moodily regarding the flowers left in his trust.

It was almost dusk, the safest hour, in between the sunlit winging of wasps and the secrecy of night. Newly armed with her driver's license, Kate got into her car and drove to Carpenter's cottage.

XIII

THE last of the light was cooler and misty, holding rain on some invisible level. When Kate reached the cottage in the first thin darkness it was like a place seen in a dream, its lights soft and wreathed at the end of the lane. Not harbor—she must not think that—but a place of detached common sense.

Kate got out of her car and walked across the dewy soundless grass to the door, rehearsing what she would say. Now more than ever she did not want to appear to throw herself on Carpenter's mercy, so she would be very brisk and careless, as if it really didn't matter much.

But it was not Carpenter who answered the door to her ring; it was a small woman with an exquisitely withered face and the commanding eyes of a tragedienne, except that they were gay instead. Carpenter's aunt, home from abroad, Kate thought instantly, and introductions proved it.

"William's out," said Mrs. Tellier, tipping her head disarmingly to one side, "but won't you come in and have a glass of sherry with me? I expect him at any minute."

Even a week ago Kate would have withdrawn at once. Now the purpose of her immediate future had become so tightly channelled that she said, "Thank you, if it isn't a bother," and stepped inside.

Mrs. Tellier, who disappeared with a murmured excuse, had left plain marks of her re-occupancy upon the cottage living room. Carpenter's winged typewriter stand, piled high with manuscript and old coffee cups and ashtrays and an occasional beer can, had been banished; in its place was a delicate Queen Anne table holding a low silver bowl of flowers. There was an unfamiliar spidery brocade chair against one wall, and a neat sheaf of opened correspondence occupied another silver bowl where Carpenter had kept his bills, memos about things he intended to insert in his copy, and anything else that came up.

". . . there," said Mrs. Tellier, reappearing with a tray. She poured sherry for both of them; tactfully, she did not glance at Kate's face as she said in an off-hand voice, "Won't you try one of those crackers? They're new to me, but they're supposed to be good . . . Tell me, how is Georgia? I called as soon as I got back, but she was out."

Kate responded automatically. Her first cracker told her that she was ravenously hungry, her first sip of sherry burned with a warning headiness. Outside, it had begun to rain.

"Joanna is fine . . ." Where was Carpenter? Mrs. Tellier deprecated the sherry, so that Kate had to finish hers with protestations. She stood up then, amazed to find that she was not quite steady, and Mrs. Tellier said, "I'm so sorry about William, I can't understand what's keeping him . . . Oh, could you wait just a minute, Mrs. Barlow? I always send Georgia some of my asters, and I wonder if you'd mind—?"

She opened a closet door, whisked herself into a raincoat, switched on an outside light, and disappeared. Kate, fighting the effects of her one glass of sherry, heard damp, grassy snapping sounds from without. Mrs. Tellier came back in with a great bouquet of rose and white and blue-purple asters; she had, she said, picked some for Kate, too. "I'll just wrap them for you—"

"Oh, don't bother. You've gone to trouble enough as it is, and I'm going straight home." Kate put out her hands to receive the flowers, but Mrs. Tellier shook her head.

"They're soaking wet, and muddy . . . there." She picked up a folded newspaper from the table beside Kate's chair, glanced at it, and said resignedly, "William's marked it, so I suppose he wants it for something—why do men mark things, instead of tearing them out then and there? But we've lots of newspapers in back, and I won't be a minute."

The rain-wet flowers had left shining, recoiling droplets on the polished table-top, and blots of dampness on the newspaper. Kate, glancing idly down, saw that Carpenter had indeed marked it; black oblique pencil strokes at the two top corners had gone partly through the paper to isolate a short item. It was impossible not to read it.

"Mailman Stung; Dies."

Kate's heartbeats gathered thickly. "A Binghamton, N.Y., postman collapsed yesterday after being stung by wasps nesting in a mailbox on a rural route. Robert B. Martinique, 39, was pronounced dead on arrival at a local hospital."

It was today's paper. But: "We've lots of newspapers in back . . ."

Kate managed to thank Carpenter's aunt for the flowers. Mindful of her sherry, carefully not thinking about anything but the road, she drove home through the rain, saw a car depart from the driveway as she neared it, and tried not to recognize it as Carpenter's. Her time sense seemed dulled, so that she did not hurry across the lawn under the crisp, solid raindrops; Georgia, exclaiming over the flowers, said alarmedly, "Kate, you're drenched!" and then, with an anxious and searching glance. "You haven't changed your mind?"

Kate stared blankly.

"About the land, I mean?"

"Oh. No."

But she had changed her mind about something else. She would take counsel with no one, except a lawyer of her own choosing, and first she would wait a necessary day.

Part of the next afternoon was occupied with the closing of the land sale; there were no complications, as everything

111

was exactly in order. Georgia, still looking disturbed, wrote a check; Kate, unnaturally calm, signed her name to a number of documents. The downtown office, with its absorbed and meticulous men, was completely impervious; destiny dwindled to nothing in this atmosphere of beige license-hung walls, soundless carpeting, special pens.

Georgia was withdrawn on the way home, and Kate's mind, travelling ahead to the finding of Barney Maynard, isolated her equally. It was not until they turned in at the driveway that Georgia, braking the blue Ford she shared with Joanna, said abruptly, "Bill Carpenter was here last night. He's quite worried about you."

Kate knew very well that Carpenter had been there, and there was no reason for the sudden rush of blood to her face. "Is he? It's kind of him, but he needn't be."

"He isn't the only one," said Georgia, tracing the wheel with a finger. She turned her head suddenly, and her usually soft blue gaze was clear and direct. "Can I help, Kate?"

She was making a communication deeper than the surface words, and to Kate it was like being invited to lie down if she were tired, or to drink if she were thirsty. But —who to trust? Georgia, who had kept the driver's license in her desk? Carpenter, who had marked out for himself a newspaper item concerning wasps? The new cool Joanna, who seemed—in Kate's mind at least—to have left a strange imprint on the apartment? Gerald . . . but however understanding he was, Gerald had all the usefulness of a rubber cane. Anything Kate told him about her plans would go instantly back to the Barlows.

Which left her alone. Perhaps irrationally, but alone. One of her gloves had seeped down between the seat cushions, so that she was able to busy herself with that and say, "Oh, I think I've got one of those hanging-on colds," without meeting Georgia's eyes at all.

The mail came elfishly late the next morning, at after eleven. An uproar of wind had followed the night's rain, chasing dark waves of cloud-shadow on the heels of brilliance, so that Kate felt safe in volunteering to go out to the black iron box clamped to the gate: wasps could hardly maneuver in this violent air.

She had thought herself forewarned and braced, but the weightless and merrily looped letter for her, postmarked Bridgeport, fell like a leaden stroke. Impervious to the whip of her dress and the spin of hair about her face, she ripped the envelope open. And there it was, the little clipping: "Mailman Stung; Dies."

Young Mr. McDermott, junior partner of McDermott and McDermott, Attorneys-at-Law, was clearly alarmed at Kate's appearance at a little after three o'clock that afternoon. Midway through what she thought was a calm and impersonal account he lifted his receiver, pressed a button, and spoke inaudibly into the phone; presently two tall glasses of iced black coffee were brought in by his secretary. Kate's heart sank at his youth and his hopeful tact, but she went on, and, when she stopped speaking, slid across his desk the newspaper clipping and the glossy print of the Maynards at the beach with the man who had called himself Dr. Sanders.

McDermott studied both with an air of wisdom and attention that looked to Kate transparently false. Of the clipping he said in a deprecating way, "Well, Mrs. Barlow, I don't know—I don't believe this is covered by any of the usual rules. It isn't obscenity, or extortion; it isn't even an anonymous letter. I know it's unpleasant, but . . ."

Of the photograph: "Doctors do take days off, and it could be argued that this is therapy for Mrs. Maynard. I know of a doctor who takes depressed patients to baseball games—sounds nutty, but he does."

He smiled humorously at Kate as he said it, but she could see the wariness in his likable pink, blue-eyed face. Well, probably she looked more in need of psychiatric treatment than Mrs. Maynard, and to anyone not steeped in the obscure and foreboding atmosphere created by Maynards' letters, which she had foolishly thrown away, the whole issue must look like a tempest in a teapot. Had the Maynards actually threatened to sue? No. Had their request for financial assistance been couched in the form of a demand? No. Well, then, why anticipate trouble?

Kate stood up, fingers clenching into her palms as desperately as though all this had been actually said aloud. "Then you don't see any point in finding the boy."

"I would think," said McDermott very cautiously, "think, mind you, that if it could be established that Mrs. Maynard never entered a nursing home—and that ought to be simple enough to check—you could dismiss the whole affair from your mind."

He did not understand at all; Kate's compulsion escaped him completely. But then, how to explain clearly the connection between a small boy on a tricycle and a horror that had begun to devour her mind? McDermott did not understand that either; as far as her obsession about wasps went, he obviously classed her with females who jumped up on chairs and screamed prettily at mice.

"I have to find him," said Kate, and only realized from the repetitive sound on the air that she had said it twice. McDermott glanced at her face and began to flip the pages of a desk calendar, frowning. "I see. Well, my father will be back from Chicago on—let's see—the twenty-ninth. I've got my hands full right now, but we ought to be able to start on it for you then."

Two weeks. To Kate, it might have been two months, but she only pulled on her gloves in silence. As though absentmindedly she picked up the photograph on the desk and slipped it into her bag. At the door, she said, "You will try the nursing homes in the meantime?" and McDermott, clearly relieved at this evidence of common sense, said that he would, and that he would also check on Dr. Sanders.

Kate drove home in her tight-windowed, airless car. Her head ached and she was drenched with perspiration by the time she reached the apartment, but before she

114

took a shower, before she did anything, she wrote a single sentence on a sheet of notepaper.

"Dear Mr. Maynard: Speaking of witnesses, I have come into possession of a recent photograph which I think might interest you."

She signed it, addressed the envelope, and forced herself back into the breathless heat of the car. Only when the letter was safely mailed did her tightness slacken even faintly.

If the Maynards were what she thought they were, surely this would flush them into the open? Even if they had seen themselves in the blurred background of the newspaper reproduction, they would have no way of knowing that was the photograph mentioned; for all they knew, Kate might have caught them far more compromisingly than that.

Although what she really wanted was not the Maynards at all, only Barney, because evidence from a dozen nursing homes could not undo the image that had transferred from glossy paper to Kate's brain: Mrs. Maynard's roguish, intensely female glance at the man Kate had met as Dr. Sanders, the bullish vitality of Maynard's flung-back head.

Had Barney been a few feet away across the sand, out of camera range? Or at home in a seethingly hot apartment, because his stutter was irritating and attention-causing?

In the silence of her own apartment, Kate faced the second alternative. The Maynards' open gate notwithstanding, she would then be linked forever with a child's damaged speech, and the faulted memory and fear that went with it. But if that was the price of certainty, it had to be paid. Apart from being turned into the very reverse of a sundial, counting only the hours of darkness, she could not live with such a question locked inside her, like a forgotten pair of scissors from an operation.

And there was a physical aspect, which struck her with mild surprise when she changed for dinner: she was gradually shrinking out of her wardrobe. Dresses she had worn only six weeks before gathered awkwardly about the waist, or hung at the shoulders, or exposed her newly thinned arms. Kate had gotten used to the change in her face, with its automatic demands for soap and water or lipstick; she was somehow startled at the dangerous slenderness of her body, and its incertitude. Joanna's vitality seemed to lie in a similar paring-down, but it was not a condition natural to Kate.

She crossed the lawn to the house to find everyone else just leaving. Joanna, incisive in black linen, lithe gold bracelet gleaming over a short black glove, said with a curious glance, "Sally Wainwright's buffet, remember? You begged off."

"Oh, that's right." But Kate did not remember.

Georgia said with a last pat at her high-dressed honey hair, "Kate dear, you look tired. Haven't you been dashing about an awful lot lately?"

"Just—enjoying being a licensed driver again," said Kate, smiling carefully. "It's wonderful—like getting citizenship papers."

A tiny silence fell. Into it, Gerald remarked unhappily that the last time he had been at the Wainwrights' he had had to fill his pockets with inedible morsels, being napkinless at the time, and that whenever he wore that suit, despite numerous cleanings, he attracted other marinated herrings. While he said it, he drooped one eyelid at Kate; the almost-wink said, "Aren't you lucky, getting out of this?"

But Kate did not feel lucky, when the sound of the car had died away. She had been in the house alone before, but never with this alien, trespassing feeling; if she had known in advance, she would have provided herself with fruit or a sandwich to eat in the apartment. But it would be singular, if only to herself, to depart from custom now, and she opened the refrigerator door automatically.

The remains of the cold lamb had a faintly defensive air, as though earmarked for curry or hash; the egg-ringed potato salad looked impossibly heavy. There was a can of tomato madrilene which Kate thought she could manage with a cracker or two, and she opened that.

How frightening that she could not remember ever hearing about the Wainwrights' buffet, let alone declining it. And how quiet the house was, mocking her when she dropped a spoon, folding into permanent record the rasping close of a drawer. The crackers, when Kate took them out of their box, re-echoed like tumbling shingles.

I'm getting peculiar, she thought lucidly, staring at the steeps and shines of the madrilene, and that would never do for Robert's wife. Of course that's why they didn't tell me about the Wainwrights.

The house seemed suddenly to explode with sound. It was only the doorbell chimes, but the soup plate fell shatteringly from Kate's hand.

XIV

CARPENTER helped her clean up the wreckage; something about his dispatch suggested that he was an accomplished dropper of plates. Smiling at her from under the front door lantern, he had said, "Hello, Kate. I knocked at your door but you weren't there," and then, hastily, as though to cover up this profundity, "Was it my imagination, or did I hear a sound of breaking crockery?"

"Yes, you did." Anger at her own instability—and at Carpenter, who had succeeded in making her think satirically, just a moment ago, "That would never do for Robert's wife"—turned Kate's voice short. In silence she turned and went into the kitchen, and Carpenter followed her.

The madrilene was almost as uncapturable as quicksilver, and there seemed enough jagged fragments of blue and white flowered china to supply a banquet table. Unadmitted on the air, but thoroughly understood, was the fact of Georgia's deep displeasure if she had been there. She was fond of her possessions, and as neat as a laboratory technician about her kitchen; with the Barlow calm and sure-handedness she would not be able to understand such clumsiness, and it was not a subject she would easily let drop. ("But I don't understand, Kate—were you balancing it on your palm, or. . . ? Oh, but you must have knocked it against something, because otherwise I don't see—")

It made a scene of ridiculous intimacy, two adults peering about the floor like guilty children, and as though he were aware of it, Carpenter did not glance again at Kate's set, white face. He said casually that his aunt had told him of Kate's visit to the cottage, and he was sorry he had been out; that, in fact, he had been here, and they must just have missed each other. Was there something he could do?

"Oh, no. As I'd made such a mess of the manuscript, and I was driving by anyway, I thought I'd ask if there were any pages you wanted retyped."

Carpenter did not reply directly. Instead, straightening with a last palmful of blue and white chips, he said, "Where do these go?"

"Oh—anywhere. Here." Georgia would see the fragments at once, but Kate did not care. She said formally, "Thank you very much," and turned away. Behind her, Carpenter made a sudden sound of exasperation, and she turned back to see him squinting at his hand and turning it under the light.

"Splinter," he said. "It's broken off."

There was a drop of blood welling at the base of one finger, and Kate came automatically close to inspect it. Instantly, Carpenter's other hand came out to close over her wrist. He said very quietly, "Kate, what the hell is all this?"

She would not wrench her hand away, she would not show him the slightest reaction although her skin burned queerly. "All what?"

"Well, that's typical," said Carpenter flatly. "Looking like the devil, and acting as though you were surrounded by hostile Indians, and still pretending everything is just fine. Or do you always drop dishes when the doorbell rings?"

Kate bit back a savage, "Yes, always," because there was a chance that he might tell her the truth. She said steadily, lifting her gaze, "I suppose I'm nervous. I got something quite unpleasant in the mail this morning."

The even pressure of his fingers did not alter. "What was it?"

"A newspaper clipping about a mailman who died from wasp stings. Sent," said Kate, still very steady, "by some

119

fond and thoughtful friend who knows how terrified I am of wasps."

Now was the time for him to say, "I sent it," or even, "I saw that in last night's paper," but Carpenter did neither. He said instead, holding her gaze innocently, "Those people, do you think? The—what was their name—Maynards?"

How right she had been not to trust him—and she could not remember having told him the Maynards' name. "Possibly," said Kate without expression.

Carpenter gave a thoughtful little frown. "What would be the point, do you suppose?"

Kate felt suddenly sickened. She released her wrist with a brusque gesture and turned away, collecting her cigarettes and matches from the table. "I don't know. I've got to get back now."

"But wasn't that your dinner we just cleaned up?"

"I wasn't really hungry."

"Come and have dinner with me," suggested Carpenter, and Kate, at the door, turned to look at him with real astonishment. After a moment she said quietly, "I don't believe I could eat."

She had never said such a thing to another human being before, but then she had never been so cruelly taunted and lied to, either. Carpenter said measuredly, "Thank you," and she could feel the quick dangerous pressure of anger in him. "You know," he said, holding the door politely for her and then closing it behind both of them. "I've wronged you. In time, I think you're going to make a very good Barlow."

"Good-night," said Kate stonily, and walked across the dark grass to her apartment. She had been inside a full minute before the door of Carpenter's car slammed with such energy that she would not have been surprised to hear it collapse into a heap of nuts and bolts. But it did not; it revved furiously and roared away.

Her head ached badly, and although it was a ridiculous hour for bed, about eight-thirty, she took an aspirin and undressed and lay staring blankly at her book. She was not hungry at all, which worried her a little in a detached way, but she thought, I'll be all right when I find Barney. Briefly, it was though a spotlight had been turned on a child's face, so that all the surrounding faces—Georgia's and Joanna's, Gerald's and Carpenter's and the Symmes'—dropped back into an uninteresting dusk.

The aspirin on an empty stomach made her drowsy, and she fell into a half-sleep with the light on. "A very good Barlow . . ." Carpenter must have hated Robert to say that. And here came a sound, the soft sound of something tracking her, almost a purr, to deceive her. It was the wasp cluster, the monstrously-drifting, locked-together organism that would seek her out and kill her—

Kate woke to the bursting pound of her heart; wild moments went by before she knew the yellow light of her room, her disordered sheets, the corner of her slipped-down book digging into her arm. There was an inquisitive fly circling her bed lamp, and the clock said ten minutes after three.

She got up, trembling, wondering on a sane deep-down level how much of this the human mechanism could stand. She drank a glass of water and smoked part of a cigarette, smoothed her sheets and turned her pillow and went back to bed. At four o'clock, knowing the after-effects and not caring, she got up again and swallowed a sleeping pill. At a little after eight, leaden with the drug, she drove to Bridgeport.

As though the mere fact that she had mailed a letter to him could summon Maynard instantly to the post office, Kate parked across the street from it. She knew that it might be a long wait—she might have to come back to-morrow, and the next day, and the next—but sooner or later Maynard would pick up his mail, and lead her to Barney. She had been naive on her earlier expedition here, thinking it to be only a matter of explaining things

121

to Maynard. Now she knew better, and she had her car. And her driver's license.

The early morning had been cool; by eleven o'clock the street was sealed with heat, the post-office steps seemed to waver a little in the shimmering air. The traffic now, after the brisk opening rush, seemed to be mainly women and elderly men, but Kate watched with steady vigilance, because what was to prevent Mrs. Maynard from picking up the mail?

At twelve o'clock she drank the last of her carton of coffee and ate the sandwich she had bought on the way. Her body felt welded to the car seat, and she got out and crossed the sidewalk to stand for a few minutes in the shade of a store awning. Instantly there was a policeman at her side, a gray-haired man with small suspicious eyes. He nodded at her car. "You—uh—waiting for somebody"

There was a parking meter, but Kate had fed it punctiliously. "Yes, I am."

"Oh," said the policeman, visibly mulling that over. "Kind of ties up that space."

"I suppose it does," said Kate, standing her ground, and after a further uncommunicative moment the policeman moved slowly away.

Kate knew that he was only doing his duty—probably dynamiters of public buildings studied the scene for quite a while before they lit the match—but his occasional glance down the street at her, from its head where he was directing traffic, added to the discomfort of her vigil. The car was stupefyingly hot, and presently she opened her window a few cautious inches.

Two o'clock came, and three, and a conviction that the Maynards had foresightedly sent a friend for their mail, or planned to. Kate did not know why she felt it so strongly, but she did. All the expectancy had gone out of the afternoon, and she knew she was going to look at an endless parade of strangers. But she could not, would not go home yet. Then where?

The Maynards had gone to the beach the other day,

but Kate stood no chance at all of finding a single small boy on such a crowded expanse. She started the car and left the post office, driving at random, trying to think.

Barney had not been present in the beach photograph, which could mean that he had been out of camera range or somewhere else entirely. At home by himself? That was a large risk with a four-year-old. Left with friends? Possibly, although in this new light the Maynards' move to Bridgeport seemed a flight to a place where they were unknown and could not easily be traced.

The Maynards—or the Mitchells?

Kate's subconsciousness must have been turning that over for some time, because the question flashed effortlessly into her mind. On her first visit to the house on Maple Avenue the woman's drowsy voice had called from another room, "Mitch . . . Mitch?" although the second time, in the presence of Sanders, she had said, "Show him the bills, Jim."

Mitch could be a private nickname between them, of course, and not the familiar shortening of Mitchell. Or the full name might be J. Mitchell Maynard. But the man's face had been transformed with worry at his wife's call, and he had bundled Kate rapidly out of the house. The use of an alias would certainly account for his anxiety that the incident should not be reported to the police.

On the other hand—and this had been the stumbling-block from the beginning—Mrs. Maynard had looked ill; not with the art of pale powder and left-off lipstick and uncombed hair, but genuinely so. And Barney hadn't been able to speak, at least then; Kate herself had seen the tremor of effort around his mouth.

The matter was of only academic interest. She was not looking for vengeance but for vindication, and a resultant release from the terror that was shaping her life into a daily more unnatural mould. But until she found Barney, and learned the truth for herself—

Kate's foot came down suddenly on the brake. Her wanderings through the city had brought her to a municipal wading pool full of small jumping shrieking children, and for seconds that suspended her breath she stared at a boy alone by the edge, a thin little boy with a round blond head. He turned as she watched, and he wasn't Barney; still, she drove on with a conscious direction and a new excitement.

How could she have forgotten the park, traditional haven for city-dwelling parents of young children? You saw the mothers in the shady green areas of every city, pursuing their offspring or calling querulously from benches according to disposition; sometimes you saw whole groups of children in the charge of one tormented-looking mother who was, presumably, earning a week's freedom of her own.

Nerves drawn tight with expectation even while she warned herself that this was too simple, that Barney would not be here, Kate found the main park. It was dauntingly crowded, and as soon as she entered she could see why: after the steady burn of the sun, this was like entering a cooled and darkened room. Part of it was the softness of grass underfoot instead of scalding pavement, part the haloes of moisture that seemed to drift down from the shielding elms. There were brilliant pokings of light, and even whole dry blazes of sun, but they only intensified the shade.

And there were children everywhere. When they were not running, they were in clusters around the drinking fountains, the ice cream cart, a popcorn stand. Kate's gaze was bemused; how, she wondered, did any parent sieve out his own child when it was time to go home?

Deafeningly close to her ear, a woman shouted, "Susan Ann, stay away from that fountain!" and like magic a drenched little girl backed out of the berry-thick clump. Kate wandered off.

She passed a good-natured fight between two boys, and something else that looked like a real settling of accounts. A girl's voice called the age-old sing-song chant, "Johnny loves Rebec—ca," and a whole stream of giggling, slapping children pelted by. Little by little, Kate grew aware of

an occasional curious glance from adult pigeon-feeders and
newspaper-readers.

There were other childless people here, but they were
young couples stretched on the grass, or older women and
men visibly grateful for the benches and the coolness. A
psycopath, thought Kate suddenly, must look very much
as she did; must walk with controlled excitement through
public places like this, glancing everywhere, studying one
face eagerly and skipping another, as though in search of
just the right child to approach, woo with candy, and
spirit away.

She had reached the end of this side of the park,
marked, inside its railings, by the statue of a city bene-
factor and a plaque set into a little knoll. Beside the plaque,
with the disordered exactness of something in a dream,
sat Barney Maynard.

XV

HIS profile flashed around with an almost animal alertness, so that Kate, who would have liked a second or two to absorb her own stunned recognition, had no time at all. Footsteps barely checked, heart thundering, she went forward and said, "Hello, Barney."

The blue eyes looked up at her, over the barest suspicion of tensing and recoil. Traffic went by, twenty feet away, but the park might have been a world locked in. The edges of Kate's vision saw no one near them under the trees, so the chances were that Barney was waiting for his parents, obediently, in spite of the alluring shouts and screams from behind him.

She said—and how amiable she sounded, like all the dangerous strangers children were forbidden to talk to— "Don't you remember me—Mrs. Barlow? I remember you. You were in bed, and you had a parakeet in your room."

The round blue stare continued. ("Barney does not remember being hit . . .")

"I owe you a tricycle," said Kate deliberately, "and if you don't want that, then I owe you something else. You'll have to pick it out, because I haven't any little boys and I wouldn't know."

And it was like a tracing falling into place over the original image: there was the look of fright she had seen in the house on Maple Avenue, the tensing of lips and throat. A feeling of terror invaded Kate; she had thought she was prepared for this, but she was not. Perhaps he couldn't speak, out of the shyness of stuttering, except in

126

the presence of familiar people. Certainly he was caught in a terror deeper than hers, because his gaze tore to the pavement beyond the railings with a wild and watchful air, as though salvation, in the form of his parents, might come at any moment.

To Kate, it was as premonitory as a footstep on a bottom stair, because how much more time had she alone with Barney? He would fly from her at a signal from the Maynards, and they would make sure that she did not find him again. She said firmly, "Barney, I know you can talk. Your father told me so."

The elms stirred faintly overhead, and that was all. "Very well," said Kate, and reached into her pocketbook and found a quarter. She had to take his hand and fold the fingers securely over it. "What do you say?"

"Thank you," said Barney.

It was a small and automatic phrase—the only reason it had slipped past his guard—but Kate's world shook with the success of her gamble. Only two words, it was true, but they had come out clearly, without a trace of stammer or even hesitation. The trees seemed greener, the air as drinkable as water, and how had she missed the faint sweetness of birds in the upper branches?

But it was still not enough. "You've been fooling me," said Kate in an admiring voice. "You could talk all the time, couldn't you?"

She realized even before the set of his mouth that she had gone too far. He was too young to think in terms of betrayal, but he would sense trouble for his parents if he admitted any deception. (And no wonder the Maynards had held their breath in the little bedroom when Kate had coaxed Barney about the tricycle; no wonder the woman had turned away with that sharp sigh—of relief, and not the despair it seemed, because involuntarily, like any small boy asked about a gift he wanted, Barney had almost answered her.)

But there was something else Kate could question him about, something that would seem to pertain only to strang-

127

ers. She dropped down beside him on the grass, so as not to seem so dauntingly tall, and noticed that he edged very slightly away. "Barney, you remember the day I came. Did somebody else come, before that?"

Barney had been watching the pavement beyond the railings with a fixity that seemed more desperate than stubborn, but at her question he turned his head just long enough to give her a glance of astonishment. The glance said unmistakably, "How did you know?" before he looked away again.

Kate's heart leaped, but cautiously. Barney had obviously related the visitor to himself, but how much had he been allowed to see or hear, and how far could she trust any identification? Because this was, had to be, the witness.

She would not make her earlier mistake. She said casually, "It was Miss Henderson from across the street, wasn't it? She's awfully nice, and she likes you very much."

"It wasn't her," said Barney, and Kate realized with a far-off amazement that although he had ruled her life for weeks it was only the second time she had ever heard him speak. (But had she heard him crying in the background, the day Sanders had called her and given off-stage instructions to "Nurse"?) Unlocked, his voice was clear and precise, with an almost adult quality disturbing at four years. "She has no car."

"Oh, that's right," said Kate, schooling herself and clenching the hands concealed by her skirt. "And this was a big black one."

"No, it wasn't. It was—"

Maddeningly he stopped there; it was as sharp and clear a stop as though he had suddenly heard an order. Was she to be balked here? He knew, he certainly knew the car. Quickly, because his preoccupation with the passers-by was contagious, and there might be almost no time left at all, Kate jumped to her feet before she could put out her arms to the thin little body or be gentle with the small embattled face.

She said coldly, "If you don't tell me about the car, I'll shake you."

It was not a face that fear became; it was instantly shamed and humbled and obedient. Kate loathed herself, and the Maynards, because her random threat, the only one she could think of, had clearly found a target. Barney had been shaken before, and cruelly; she put that by to remember.

But he stood, breaking his tense knees-up posture for the first time, and took a careful look at the cars lining all sides of the park. Kate's nerves tied themselves quietly into knots, because he had only to offer her a car, any car, to be rid of her. On the other hand, he was still frightened; he did not know what violence she might commit at a lie.

"Like that car," said Barney with relief, and pointed at a blue Ford coupe.

He sounded very certain, but that might be unconscious; you saw blue Ford coupes everywhere. And how reliable was he, at his age?

"With a lump in the door I get out of," said Barney firmly.

By the time Kate had figured that out, she could command her voice; could say, "Oh yes—of course," as though she had known it all along, and even grope for and find a cigarette and matches in the depths of her pocketbook. She could not remember wanting a cigarette with such urgency. "If your father and mother don't like you to talk to people in the park, Barney, you don't have to say I was here."

He did not even glance at her. Like a marionette with its strings cut, he dropped back into his original stoical pose: striped-jersey back against the little knoll, arms clasped about his knees.

There was one more vital thing. "Where do you live now, Barney?"

"In a house."

129

"Yes, but where? Do you know the name of the street? I'd like to send you a letter now and then."

Children of that age seldom knew street names, but then Barney was not the usual child of his age. Kate held her breath, and Barney said, "By the smokestack. There's trailers."

His voice had changed; it was unwilling and almost inaudible. Kate said gently to the top of his head, "Then I'll come and see you some time, if I may. Good-bye," and got no response at all. She walked away, amazed at her own steadiness, and looked back. He was still sitting there, braced and quiet, like a child in a corner. There was no sign of the Maynards anywhere, and no reason why she should feel watched.

The park was beginning to empty as she left; children had begun to cry tiredly, babies wanted their bottles. Kate walked the three blocks to her car with the unreal everydayness of someone who has just learned a final verdict from the doctor.

A blue Ford coupe, the witness had come in, with a dent in the passenger door. Joanna's car was a blue Ford coupe, and it had been dented weeks before in a parking lot. In the shadows cast by a street light—and the Maynards' summons to Kate on the day after the accident argued that the "witness" had turned up the evening before —the dent would have looked very like a lump.

All three of them drove the car: Joanna, and Gerald, and Georgia. Which of them had gone secretly off in it that night they all pretended to calm Kate, said to the Maynards, "I saw the whole thing," armed them with their weapon, watched with satisfaction Kate's gradual dissolution?

And why?

All at once, like a signal, Georgia's remembered voice said, "That land has already appreciated, and it might go a lot higher. . ."

How high?—although that was an academic question now. Except that they were, thought Kate for the first time, money-loving people in an unobtrusive way. Gerald had an artless loathing of any kind of work. Joanna, in understandable expectation of the Symmes' inheritance, would find it extremely unpleasant to have to study dress-shop price tags or the right-hand side of dinner menus. And surely Georgia's hours over the house accounts, and her preoccupation with the electric-light and telephone bills, argued a refusal to return to the necessitous mining-camp days.

Or was it—the money—tied to hatred like an extra tail to a kite, just to make it the more worth flying?

Carpenter knew, thought Kate suddenly, or at least suspected: it was implicit in his urgings that she move from the apartment and separate herself completely from the Barlow household. Even his evasiveness about the news-paper clipping he had marked for his own attention—"The Maynards, do you suppose?" and "What would be the point?" seemed now a deliberate prod, as though he had said, "Wait a minute. Think who might be doing this to you, and why."

But that would mean—her mind had to stumble to it, laboriously—that he suspected someone in the house of sending the clippings; he didn't know about the letters. And if he was right, had the letters with their requests for money and veiled implications come from J. Maynard at all? You could establish any identity at a General Delivery in a strange post office, and you would certainly be care-ful not to pick up your mail when your victim's car was gone from the driveway . . .

It was Georgia who had kept the driver's license; re-member that.

Feeling like a stranger in her own car, Kate drove steadily and carefully toward home. At a motel on the out-skirts of town, she stopped, went into the office, and en-gaged a room. Almost without effort she wrote her middle and maiden names, Anne . McNeill, added "Morningside Drive" at random, left the space for telephone blank.

But it was odd how awkward an impersonal deception

could make you feel. Kate, her face flushed, had to remove almost everything from her pocketbook before she could find her wallet; she must look, she thought wildly, as though she had hired a room for immoral purposes.

The clerk inspected her registration card elaborately, and picked up a pen. "*Miss?*" he inquired with emphasis.

Kate had removed her wedding ring a week ago, because with the new thinness of her hands it kept slipping off. "Yes."

But the indentation on her finger was there, unmistakably. "I'll send someone to help with your bags," said the clerk smoothly.

"No—thank you, I'll be coming in a little later."

Kate took her key and turned away, head militantly up. Almost out of the little office she paused, found a dime in her change purse, and slipped into the phone booth just inside the door. Carpenter might not be able to answer this for her, but he could give her some sort of guide—

Carpenter's phone rang emptily back at her.

Kate was shocked at her own sharp sense of loss; it was as though she had always supposed that he would be there when and if she needed him. Behind her at the desk, as she left, a heavy man in sunglasses was registering, and a frail-looking woman, face stamped with patience, was saying to a whining child, "Yes, I told you, as soon as Daddy sees the man."

Kate drove back to the apartment, comforted by the motel key in her pocketbook. The long gray house looked eerily the same, as though it did not harbor a killing purpose, and Gerald was out on the lawn digging unenthusiastically at weeds with a V-shaped implement. At Kate's approach he sneezed violently and brightened. How nice and lazy he was, she thought removedly; how "un-Barlow-like."

"Kate," said Gerald rapidly, before she could be appalled at herself, "come in and suggest a drink, quickly." He sneezed again. "This is killing me."

"Why are you weeding all of a sudden?"

"Oh, we're going on vacation tomorrow—Joanna's got it into her head that she can't wait another day—and Georgia says the lawn is full of . . . I don't know, something." said Gerald, gazing discouragedly about him. His glance came back to Kate's face. "You look rather feeble. Where've you been?"

"In Bridgeport," Kate added on impulse, "How did you come to get your vacation after all?"

Gerald gazed stealthily about him. "Simple—but don't tell Georgia, it's part of the bargain. Do you know where my father met Mrs. Holden? She was a waitress at a lodge in Vermont, and apparently—" he waggled his eyebrows significantly "—she was involved in some scandal there, a suicide, I think. Vermont must be a very grim place to shoot yourself in. The trial comes up in about three weeks, and as Mrs. Symmes," Gerald said it matter-of-factly "she won't, around here, be forced to testify. Joanna found it out, though, and it's worked wonders. What were you doing in Bridgeport?"

Trust Gerald, who was looking at her so kindly? "Oh, this and that," said Kate vaguely, and Gerald plunged his weeder firmly into the lawn and said, "Well, come in and make a diversion."

Kate went in, feeling unreal. Joanna was washing lettuce in the kitchen; she smiled a welcome. Gerald busied himself with ice and glasses, and presently Georgia came downstairs. She said in a general tone, "Hasn't it been a day?" and to Kate, "You look awfully tired. You really ought to get away."

How solicitous they all were . . . Kate was physically grateful for her drink; reaction, and the knowledge of consuming hatred behind at least one pair of kind and familiar eyes, had turned her suddenly nerveless. But she must sit as though it were any other evening, until she could get away safely; she must conceal her farewell feeling about this room and the people in it.

She did look, but only once, at the liquid in her glass. There would be no such crudity, she knew that instinctively. Dead, she would be no pleasure to anyone; it was the demoralizing effects of guilt and terror that were so enjoyable—such as her involuntary start when the telephone rang.

Georgia talked earnestly to someone about a meeting of the Welfare Committee. Coming back to the couch, she said, "Oh, Kate, before I forget—Bill Carpenter called this afternoon and said to tell you good-bye and good luck and so on."

For a mad second it was as though Kate's motel key lay exposed to everyone. Then Georgia said, "He's off to New York, it seems—something about his book. I must say I don't envy him in this weather."

Kate managed to say calmly that she didn't either, but the finality of that "good-bye and good luck" was oddly chilling. Well, of course he would have nothing further to say to her—he had been generous, at that, to someone whose last words to him had been as biting as she knew how to make them.

The telephone rang again, and Joanna was nearest. She said after a listening moment, "I see . . . Yes, thank you, I'll tell her," and turned to Georgia, putting down the receiver. "Marian Camp, at the Stocking Shop—your stockings have come in."

"Oh, good, I'll pick them up tomorrow. I ordered some for you, by the way, they wear like iron."

Am I, wondered Kate, then and during dinner, really out of my mind? She had read somewhere that a paranoiac phase could follow shock—such as the near-fatality with Barney Maynard—and produce tales of intricate and very believable plots against the victim. Because across from her, more like Robert than ever in the flickering definition of candlelight, Joanna was saying something idle about needing a new beach robe; Georgia was equally idle about a sale at the Surf Shop; Gerald, poking thoughtfully at his plate, observed to Kate without rancor that cream sauce must be very good if you liked it. Where was the concentration of venom now?

THE WASP

Suppose—just suppose—that Barney had been mute for a time, had stuttered, had recovered. Suppose that the Maynards, moved equally by bitterness and greed, had sent all the communications to Kate. Joanna's was surely not the only blue Ford coupe with a dent in the passenger door, even in this little town . . . In Kate's confused and turned-about mind, this placed her as a neurotic, and someone with whom they had all been heroically patient.

The night was surprisingly black when she crossed the lawn to the · apartment, because in going straight to the house she had not left a lamp burning against her return. Kate groped for her key in the darkness, didn't find it, and turned on her car headlights for a further unavailing search. It was undoubtedly where she had left it at least twice before, on the coffee table in front of the couch. She had lost the duplicate in the first week of her tenancy, and never gotten around to having another copy made.

It was a nuisance, but only that. The windows were low, and Kate always left the screen in her bedroom unhooked for just such an emergency. Not three minutes later, slightly breathless from her scramble over the sill, she was standing in the bedroom.

With something newly sticky smeared on her right instep and the toe of her navy calf pump.

Kate bent and put a finger to the stickiness. After moments, or possibly whole minutes, without turning on any light other than the bedside lamp she had lit on entering, she unbolted the back door and went out into the dark.

She was not out of her mind, and she had not simply imagined that thick conclave of bees and wasps around the apartment. The underside of every windowsill was thickly coated with honey.

XVI

KATE packed with frantic calm.

She had to resist a physical impulse to run, because with her already badly depleted resources she could not very well commence a new existence in only the clothes she wore. Besides, there were the semi-official things: checkbook, bank statements, income tax papers, other burdening documents accumulated over the years. She was not coming back here.

But nothing had changed, outwardly. The honey had been there—how long? Since the first time she had shown terror at the sight of a wasp?—and it was only by the most freakish chance that she had discovered it. No; the situation was as it had been before, except that her mind backed off, appalled, from such a tortuous scheme for inducing fear in another human being.

Bottom drawer of her bureau now: scarves, sweaters, a picture of herself and Robert in Arizona, which she had not been able to look at when she came to the apartment. She looked at it now, and Robert's face was a stranger's —but not a stranger's, really. Joanna's, translated into the masculine. Quietly, very much aware of what she was doing, Kate dropped the photograph back and closed the drawer.

She had two medium-sized suitcases, and an overnight case; she was almost ready to go. Bureau and closets and bathroom medicine cabinet were stripped, and all that remained was the drawer in the small table Kate had used when she wrote letters. Pulling it open, she had the sharp strange sense of a moment lived through before—but she was mistaken, because there was nothing in the drawer that mattered: an old bank statement, a box of picture-hangers, an announcement from the laundry that they would deem it a privilege to "Ice-olate" her furs.

Scrupulously, Kate left the picture-hangers.

Lastly, a note, because she did not want a hue and cry raised, deliberately or in all innocence. After some unproductive thought, she wrote: "Georgia—Took your advice and decided on a week-end away. See you Monday, Kate."

It was not very good; it was all her numbed mind could think of as a delaying action. And now there was nothing to do but wait until the faint sprawls of radiance from the lighted windows of the house winked off the dark lawn.

Fortunately they were early retirers; by ten o'clock the night was black and still. Kate got up, as stiff as someone who had sat for hours on a waiting-room bench, made two trips to the car with her suitcases. Her mind did not run on ahead, because all she required from the immediate future was safety. With a new caution that fitted her as closely as a chill, she pulled the door of the apartment quietly closed on the note, so that it fluttered free.

She did not start the car, nor even shut the door securely behind her, because the dark house was like a dangerous animal, lightly asleep. There was just enough slope to the driveway to carry her slowly and silently down to the road with the brake released, and she waited perhaps two minutes for the heavy ground-shaking hum of a truck to cover the catch of the ignition. The house windows were still dark and silent, patched peacefully with moonlight, but at the corner Kate drew up and looked tensely into her rearview mirror.

No light flashed on, no headlights came curving out after her. She was presumed to be sleeping, unaware of the lure of honey on her windowsills, innocent of the virulence so very close to her.

She was safe.

She might once have thought this motel room shabby, but now it seemed all that anyone could want. It was around the corner from the lighted office, so that her car sank into an anonymous dark, and its door locked securely, its curtained windows were high in the walls. Bed, night table with telephone, tiny desk with a chatty memo under glass: a whole new little world, and her own.

Kate still did not think ahead. She unpacked the suitcase with immediate things—nightgown, toothbrush and toothpaste—and hung two dresses in the closet. She felt dazed, as though she had won a race but could not get her breath back, and when she had aimlessly smoked a cigarette, to establish her tenancy, she drew a deep hot bath and got into it. She was so tense that she shuddered now and then even under the lapping heat, but by keeping her attention on the smoked faucets and the sweated tile just above the bathtub rim, she grew gradually calmer. She was Anne McNeill here, not Robert's wife, not hated. She was secure.

In the bedroom, like a knife ripping through her calm, the telephone rang.

The room clerk, to find out whether she had arrived? Or her enemy? She had felt watched in the park with Barney, and if she had been followed here on her first stop this afternoon—

The telephone stopped. The clerk at the switchboard had said mechanically to the caller, "I'm sorry, there is no answer."

Kate got out of the tub and dried herself in a consciously careful silence, as though the black instrument in the bedroom had some sly and secret way of noting and transmitting her presence here. When she went back in, it looked visibly imminent, like a cat on the point of meowing, or a child about to cry.

To what, she thought in horror, have I been reduced? Although the small, misted bathroom mirror had given her a partial answer to that. In her new removedness, she realized that she would be unrecognizable to people she had known a year ago; passing her on the street, or dining at a neighboring restaurant table, they might say to each other, "That looked a little like Kate McNeill . . . something, I don't know what . . ."

It was not only the physical change, the piercing thinness; almost as much, it was the presence of fear and uncertainty—the defensive bracing of the shoulders, the hand wandering blindly out to an ashtrayed cigarette, the unnatural alertness to innocent sounds. The very picture of a woman harboring a deep and unadmitted guilt.

Kate turned her back on the telephone, knowing even that to be weakness, and found a reprint in her suitcase. Behind her, triumphantly, the telephone rang.

It was a battle—there were five long steady rings, seeming to electrify every fiber of wood and fabric in the room before they stopped—but she won. And surely, now, she would seem not to be here?

But her car, standing out there in darkness, perfectly recognizable to anyone who knew it—

To Kate, standing with guarded tensity while the echoes of the phone died away, the night seemed suddenly full of sinister metallic sounds. Then, startlingly close to her windows, a woman's voice said peevishly, "I told you you should have gotten out his teddy bear before dinner, you know he won't sleep without it."

Kate relaxed, tinily, at the slam of a car door, the receding footsteps, the man's placating, "All right, all right, I got it, didn't I?"

She was in bed, the familiar tick of her travelling clock sounding at her shoulder, when the knock came at the door.

It was smart and purposeful, not a knock to be denied even if the lighted windows did not betray her wakefulness. Something about it suggested that if Kate did not reply a master key would be produced and that the door would be opened while she cowered in the farthest corner.

A buried forethought had made her keep her robe on, so that she was not quite as vulnerable as someone caught in a nightgown. At the second knock, and the called, "Miss McNeill? You in there?" Kate sat higher against her pillows, muscles braced, and called back, "What is it?"

"I got a message for you. I rang your room and then I figured you might be in the tub." It was a boy's voice, cocky, not quite impudent. "Somebody called but didn't leave their name. And the child had to be punished, so they locked him up."

Child: not his wording, Kate knew instinctively; he would have said "kid." Although her fingers had clenched into her palms she said coolly through the door, "What child?"

"I d'know, I just come on."

"Was this all one message, or two?"

Pause. "It doesn't say here on the slip," said the boy as though he were examining something in a dim light.

She had never heard his voice before tonight, but still —"Would you mind sliding it under the door?" said Kate, and the ridiculous exchange took place, laboriously; a corner of white paper came twitching through just as her fifty-cent piece disappeared. "Thank you," said the boy, and she tried not to think it mocking.

The slip was uninformative, scribbled with ink under the printed "Messages." It said, "Call for McNeill, No. 14, no answer," and then, starkly, "Child had to be punished so they locked him up."

Barney. Punished for talking to her in the park. Locked up—

No, thought Kate, taking a long breath. This was a very clumsy maneuver, almost to have been expected—the mention of a threat to Barney so that she would rush from cover and expose herself to whatever was planned. Oh, no indeed. Deliberately, she tossed the slip of paper into the wastebasket and got back into bed.

She turned a page of her book grimly, but it did not

disturb the superimposed image of Barney's wary young face, and the terror with which he had kept glancing out at the street. Terror of her—or of retribution if he were seen talking to her? He was certainly no stranger to physical violence. Kate turned another page, to convince herself that she was reading, and found herself staring past the edge of it at a fold of bedspread.

The message was a trick, obviously. Whoever hated her thought that she knew where Barney lived, and danger waited for her there. There was not one chance in a hundred that he was being cruelly punished on her account.

But when she had admitted the one chance in her mind, it grew so dominant that it paled the other ninety-nine. Having deceived Kate from the beginning, the Maynards would be both frightened and angry if they discovered that Barney had talked to her in the park, and fear was an even sharper goad than anger.

And there was Kate's enemy, the "witness," the dreadful patience that had set out to destroy her. How could the witness be sure how much a little boy in an upstairs room had seen and heard—and said? If it were the witness who had observed that interval in the park . . .

The Barlows and the Symmes' had always lived in the town with their heads high; they were civic as well as social lights. The lawyer had told Kate that the newspaper clippings were not actionable, and there was certainly no statute to cover the smearing of honey on windowsills. But conspiracy to defraud—and defraud Robert Barlow's widow—would be something else again. Suppose that, and all the venomous little tricks, should be exposed through the agency of a small boy?

"The child had to be punished—" Oh, God. What, just possibly, had she done to Barney while she saved herself?

Kate was suddenly damp in the air-conditioned room. "Locked him up," the message had said. Locked him up where? In a closet, a cellar, some place that he especially feared? You read occasionally of vindictive punishments of children, ending in injury and sometimes death. Would there be one last newspaper item to look at: "Boy Suffocates in Closet" . . . "Boy Strangles in Attempt to Escape From Cellar"?

The police. Kate thought of that with a sudden saving calm, and had the telephone receiver in her hand when she realized how such a report would be received and put it slowly down again. A desk sergeant would start methodically with the boy's name.

Barney Maynard, or maybe Mitchell.

Address?

By the smokestack; there were trailers.

After a significant tapping of his head at anybody else in sight at his end of the line, the desk sergeant might continue patiently:

Just how was the boy being mistreated?

Well—she had received a message that he was locked up.

Message from whom?

She didn't know.

The boy was being punished, was that it?

Yes, but—

Stoically, her tired and frightened body crying out bitterly against her mind, Kate got out of bed and dressed. A voice over the telephone was one thing to the police; a flesh-and-blood woman with credentials was another. If she went there and told them the whole thing she might make them understand, and the police had ways of locating people that ordinary citizens did not.

She put away, because she had to, the knowledge that childless widows must make up a large percentage of the women who meddled with other people's children and complained about their treatment. A little over an hour after she had entered it, she left her sanctuary and went out into the dark.

XVII

THE night was surprisingly cool, almost chilly after the burn of the day. People who drew their nightmare on chosen occasions from television or the movies strolled in and out of the motel office and attached restaurant and bar, and their light voices flickered out unreally at Kate. "Honey, Barb said Route 128—" and "Look at Joe. Honestly, give that man one drink . . . !" and from Joe, turgidly, "Well, maybe a small one."

Kate had locked her car, but before she got in she sent a combing glance around the interior. Then she swung out into the traffic bound for Bridgeport.

Normally she did not care for night driving, particularly at this hour when the drive-in movies got out and traffic went at a fairly fast but hemmed-in speed in both directions. Tonight, she felt accompanied and guarded by the steadily moving parade of lights. She had time to think what she would say—and she would have to say all of it, there was no way out of that. If only she had gone to the police in the beginning, Maynard's plea notwithstanding—

And what peril it was possible to fall into, on a quiet country road, simply because at a certain second in time a child flashed through an open gate. Everything had stemmed from that.

The traffic began to weave irritably. Kate glanced at her own speedometer and the regulation forty-five miles an hour, and stayed on the inside lane. A pale convertible swept past her, cutting in dangerously soon; she was unable

143

to brake because of a car close behind her and another coming up fast on the outside lane. Somewhere in the back distance another driver was growing annoyed at the dodging; a horn began to sound.

Gradually, the lights that had seemed so companionable took on a crowding aspect; this was a dictated pace, from which there could be no sudden deviation without a pile-up. Kate commenced to slacken speed very slightly, just enough so that people with cross sleepy children to put to bed would start to swear and edge out around her.

They did, and although one stubborn pair of headlights continued to dazzle in her rear-view mirror some of the tension of her grip on the wheel began to ease. What would have waited for her at the Maynards', provided she had known the address and been simpleminded enough to go there? Not bodily violence, or at least not to her. Some deeper involvement with the life of a small boy, some shocking new assault on her mind and conscience?

She had her wedding ring in her pocketbook; she must remember to put that on before she entered the police station, as she did not look like Mrs. anyone in her bare-fingered state, much less someone who bore the respected name of Barlow . . . and the air vent must be open, because particles of dirt were beginning to swirl about under the dashboard.

Wishing that the car behind would not press her so closely, Kate put out a hand to the air-vent knob. It was in "in" position, but the skin of her legs felt newly sensitized, almost as though there were threads dangling from the hem of her hastily pulled-on dress. Eyes on the road, left hand firm on the wheel, she bent a little and swept her right hand at her skirt edge.

A needle met it, piercing, white-hot, seeming to quiver deep under the skin. Kate snatched her hand away and knew even before the throbbing pain that she had been stung. At a feathery crawl on her instep, a further crawl along her left ankle, there was a thunderous bolt of recognition in her heart, stopping her lungs, blurring all her faculties.

It was not dust swirling up from around the floor pedals. Her car was full of wasps.

For the briefest flash—perhaps the length of time it took a wasp to sting—the car faltered and veered a little under the wild instinctive recoil of all Kate's nerves and muscles. As though she were looking at herself from some high detached place, she knew that she was going to die as Robert had died, in a smash, to wipe the slate clean.

But her hands were back on the wheel, steadyingly, and her foot touched the brake in repeated warning to the car behind, which rode so close that Kate was bathed in radiance. The driver did not notice or respond, but then he could not know about this unleashed horror, nor hear her fast half-sobbing breaths with the broken prayers in between.

The calf of her right leg burned fierily, almost obscuring a fresh thrust of venom just above the ankle. Stop, trusting to the other driver's brakes—but just then a youth on a bicycle came wheeling out of a side street. Kate's instincts steered away from him, and as though it had been in tow the other car followed.

She was not driving, she was being driven. Hounded to a faster speed, herded to destruction against another car, a telephone pole, the stanchions of a bridge . . .

She must not look down to see how many delicately-jointed legs were prowling excitedly across her lap or attaching themselves briefly to the upholstery. If she were to save herself—it was as roaring a thought as the rush of the night past her—she must put on a sudden burst of speed, pull away, dive into the first spot between the cars of night-shift factory workers ranked along the streets.

She cried out aloud at a fresh burst of pain in her left wrist, struck at the spot, and signalled imploringly with her brakes. In almost the same instant she put her foot down hard on the accelerator and pulled far enough away to recognize the car behind her.

Joanna's Ford. With someone sexless and . . . cowled at the wheel, the head silhouetted by the lights of the heedless oncoming traffic.

. . . And here was a bridge, with a dark sand-lipped mouth opening just before it on the right. Kate swung into it, whole body gasping and pounding with pain, and felt the car plummet over unexpectedly rough terrain. Marsh grass hurled up in front of her headlights, bitter green and knife-sharp, and then something larger, something connected with the underpinnings of the bridge. Mustn't hit that—

But she did, because the wheels would not respond sharply enough in the sand. She felt her head snap forward against the wheel, and then her mother was saying decisively, "George, we cannot come here for any more summers. Katherine eats the sand, and it can't be good for her . . ."

"You're dying," said someone unrelated to Kate. "Like Robert. Oh, they said he died at once, but how do they know?"

Kate lifted her stunned head from the wheel. The darkness went on rocking around her, further unsteadied by the throaty call of frogs and the dim unreal sound of traffic humming unconcernedly over the distant bridge. The wasps seemed to be gone, perhaps because her door hung open. With difficulty, she focussed her eyes on her near enemy, the witness.

She saw the witness as the Maynards must have seen her: unrecognizable. An old woman kerchiefed in a thrusting shell of dull black, the bone-pale face inside it lashless and browless, the mouth a twist. Even then, with her legs and one wrist on fire with pain and a trickle of something thicker than perspiration running from her temple to her cheek, Kate felt an incredulous pity.

She said effortfully, "Georgia, you're wrong. Robert . . ."

She had neither the breath nor the concentration to finish that, but it didn't matter. Georgia—old woman in a painstakingly youthful skin, or young mother trapped in a growing net of age?—was there to talk and watch, not to listen.

"Did you know," said Georgia in a whisper, "that Robert nearly died once, in a fire in our summer cabin? I went in after him and I saved his life, although I couldn't save my husband's. Robert owed me that—his life. He knew it, he always knew it, until he met you."

Was this, wondered Kate sickly, the much-vaunted and equally much-feared "mother love"? The hold which would not let go, the fierce possessiveness strengthened, in this case, by an incident which her child could not even have remembered? This was not love; it was exactly what Georgia had said: ownership. If you owned a race horse, you got the winner's stakes. If you owned a play, you got the royalties. If you owned a son . . .

(God help Robert's wife.) A twist of blood wound sickeningly into the corner of Kate's mouth, and she wiped it away with the wrist that was not still pounding with venom. She said over the frogs and the three feet of half-lit darkness that separated them, "I swear to you, Georgia, Robert was driving when—"

"That's a lie," said Georgia passionately. Her face went completely naked. "I know how it happened, because Robert sent me a postcard that very morning. 'It's so warm,' he said, 'that believe it or not there was a wasp in the car this morning.' I must have put a wasp in your car a dozen times—didn't you ever wonder why we were suddenly using matchboxes instead of paper folders? They're very handy for trapping wasps—and I finally proved it. Don't sit there and tell me you didn't kill Robert."

She took a step closer, and there was something at her side, not quite behind her back. Kate's muscles tensed through her pain, because Georgia meant to kill her. An animal instinct made her drop her head with its warm striping blood back against the car seat, lift it again, say, "Georgia, I can't see!"

"I told you you were dying," said Georgia coolly, "and by the time they come back with a doctor you'll be dead. Like Robert. Nobody will be surprised, because you've looked like a maniac lately, and if a wasp flew into your car after that sad, sad accident with the little boy, you'd naturally crash. And if that lawyer you hired raises any questions, I've got a sheet of your handwriting, with Mrs. Robert Barlow written in all kinds of ways, to show that you wrote those letters to yourself."

That was the strangeness Kate had felt in the apartment after Joanna left it, that was the puzzled remembrance over the drawer in the small table she had used as a writing desk. She gathered her cloudy strength, because Georgia had some kind of weapon hidden at her side, and then she remembered the earlier and betraying words: ". . . by the time they come back with a doctor . . ."

So there had been, out of all that traffic, a witness, a curious bystander. Georgia would not dare—

Except that she was completely out of control, and it was all the more frightening because she showed no physical evidence of it.

"Did you think," said Georgia with perfect calm, her face close to Kate's, "that you could live, and even—remarry, after *Robert* was dead? Oh, I tested you with Bill Carpenter, I wanted to see. The pair of you were like animals, just waiting for Robert's money before you went ahead."

She had slipped over the edge at last, because there was no question of Robert's money. "The land," said Georgia, poking her black-shelled face close to Kate's and smiling. "Remember? You don't sit on committees, you despise them, so you wouldn't know about the new highway going through, and the new shopping center. On about September fifteenth, the land you sold me will be worth at least fifty thousand instead of five."

The figures rolled incomprehensibly inside Kate's head. She sat still and quiet, because in her rear-view mirror there was a very faint golding, as though someone had turned off the road after them. The gold began to grow. Georgia seemed suddenly angered by her lack of response; she said with a whisking movement of her right hand, "Do you know what I've got here? Smelling salts. I'm going to jam your brains out against this wheel, and then I'm going to try and revive you."

She leaned into the car, a succoring figure from a distance. Kate's mind was dazzled by the pain of her stings and the almost hypnotic composure of Georgia's voice: this —this iron hand at the back of her head—was the Barlow strength, praiseworthy and perfectly lucid, except in one area.

She gripped the wheel with all her own strength, but it was not enough to combat that driving force. As her head went forward more blood trickled into her mouth, and everything was suddenly so brilliant that the light on steering wheel and gear shift and dashboard seemed to have a cutting edge. Georgia's leaning shadow was a distorted black—and then it was gone, in an incomprehensible tangle of men's voices.

The closest voice—how could it be Carpenter's, when he was in New York?—said shakily, "Kate, *Kate,*" but not even that, not even the arm that came hard around her shoulders, could obliterate the sounds of the night. Wrapped in a shell of tensity, Kate heard the shouted, "She's heading for the road!" and an answering shout, and then the long skidding scream of brakes, and the shock of silence as all traffic stopped.

XVIII

"I'm all right," said Kate blankly to Carpenter, and, presently, a state policeman and an ambulance driver, but she was taken to the hospital anyway. There, they seemed less concerned with the cut at the side of her head than with her pulse and the inner sides of her eyelids. "Shock," she heard someone say—and perhaps that was why she had not battled with Georgia, that was why she had been almost willing to accept the killing blow.

Carpenter was allowed to see her for all of a minute and a half, while a nurse stood in the doorway of the room where she had been efficiently stripped, clothed in a hospital gown, given a hypodermic, and tucked into a tight white bed. Neither of them mentioned Georgia's name. Kate said out of utter exhaustion. "I did it. The car was full of wasps, and I drove it."

"You did. You've set yourself free," said Carpenter, but his voice sounded empty and his face was not his usual half-cheerful, half-cynical face. Kate's mind groped wearily after that, until she remembered and turned her head on the pillow. "Barney—?"

"Barney's okay. Don't worry about him," said Carpenter, and turned abruptly away. "Have a good sleep, Kate."

Certainly that was nothing to cry about, but tears felt childish and luxurious, and warming on her tight cold face. By the time the first few drops had rolled across the bridge of her nose and into the pillow, Kate was asleep.

They let her go the next day. Kate had carefully avoided a morning newspaper, but the nurses had not; curious glances followed her down the hall, past the second-floor desk, into the elevator. "Barlow," said a hushed whisper. "Under a truck—trying to get help . . ."

Kate walked steadily out of the elevator and across the lobby. On the far side of it, like the firm ground you must watch unswervingly if you were to get safely across a rotten bridge, was Carpenter. He was wearing a raincoat and carrying one for her, and as she came up to him he said intuitively, "This will be short for you, it's my aunt's. All set?"

"I must have a bill somewhere."

"You can settle with me later. Now," said Carpenter, "they wouldn't let me park in front of the door, so would you like to take a creaky back elevator or walk about thirty feet to the car?"

Kate glanced past him at the streaming panes of the lobby, the dimly-glimpsed motion of branches. "Can we walk?"

It was a noisy splashing rain, gurgling and rebounding everywhere, dyeing the heat-dusted trees a glistening green and black. As Kate had known it would, it blew away the film of half-numbness that had surrounded her and restored a reality that had to be looked at, understood, and then, if it were possible, forgotten.

She said in an even voice as she reached the car, "Was Georgia killed, last night?"

"Yes. My aunt's at the house now, helping Joanna about arrangements, and I thought that you might like to come to the cottage for a very quiet drink. Incidentally," said Carpenter, frowning at the ignition and talking rapidly, so as not to give her much time to think about that swift untidy annihilation, "conclusions were jumped to last night. People assumed that Georgia got panicky when she was trying to revive you, thought you were dying, and ran for help without looking where she was going. I didn't know what you'd want," he started the car and scrupulously did not look at her, "so I let it go."

The windshield wipers began to carve clean precise arcs out of the drunken landscape. "I'm so glad," said Kate, and leaned back against the seat and closed her eyes briefly. She said, "Yes, please," when Carpenter asked her about a cigarette, and after that neither of them spoke until they reached the cottage.

It looked different in the rain, isolated and strange, but then Kate felt that way herself. Only a mile or two away Joanna was making arrangements for her mother's funeral . . . she had taken the sheet of experimental handwriting from Kate's apartment, but had she known what Georgia planned? Yes, almost certainly, and therefore the hurried departure for vacation. She wouldn't—almost Robert's twin —interfere, but she hadn't wanted to be around.

What was difficult to grasp was the stark fact that Georgia would not have let Robert's wife escape her at any cost. When her pair of casual opportunists, the Maynards, had fled, she had moved into their names and their place, attacking Kate financially as well as emotionally. First had come the comparative nibble of eight hundred and fifty dollars, then the mention of a witness and a lawsuit which had stripped Kate of her land. Two birds with one stone, really, because by the same means Kate had been reduced to a state where she could never have left her shell and earned her own living.

With the icy glass that Carpenter handed her, she was able to take a fleeting look at what her predictable future would have held: a growing uncertainty as to her ability to face the outside world, an eventual servitude to Georgia. ("Yes, that's Robert's wife. She was a very attractive girl, but she never got over his death, poor thing . . .")

Might she, in time, have come to accept guilt for having survived Robert, become grateful even for servitude as long as she was safely cloistered away? She would not have believed the possibility, even three months ago; now it seemed a pit which she had sidestepped by the merest chance. She had lost her apartment key, and discovered the smearing of honey on her windowsills—the close sweet breath of hatred.

. . . Lost her key. At the only possible place, the counter in the motel office where she had had to pile things while she dug so shakenly for her wallet under the clerk's knowing eyes. She had obviously left something else, too, something that bore her telephone number—and the phone had rung twice after her return to the house. That was how Georgia had known where to leave the message about Barney, and where to follow Kate from.

Barney, the immediate pivot of the whole thing. Kate put her glass down hard; she said wildly to Carpenter, "I forgot about Barney. God knows what . . . he may be —" and Carpenter stilled her forward rise.

"Barney's all right—you can see him any time you want. If you liked, we could even—"

He stopped there as suddenly as though he had tripped over a wire. Tensely, Kate watched him swallow half his drink, heard him say in a completely irrelevant voice, "Georgia served on an awful lot of committees, you know. Child Welfare, Public Health, Foundling Society—the whole bunch. The information she got about Barney and the Maynards was the purest luck. She would probably have managed anyway, but as things stood it was given to her on a platter."

Kate went on staring at him; she could not have spoken.

"Barney is an orphan, in the care of the state," said Carpenter evenly, "and the Maynards—actually their name was Mitchell and there was some doubt about the death of a state child they had cared for once—are paid a certain sum each month for his support. Mrs. Maynard is an alcoholic."

Rain fled across the windows, bushes scraped in the drive of wind. How clear it was, Kate thought stunnedly, when you knew; how exactly everything fell into place. Barney's mute obedience on that first day: not the obedience of love or trust, but of fear because he had left the gate open. Maynard's insistence that Kate should not notify the police, Mrs. Maynard's blurry voice from the bedroom, the perfume and pine scent, disguising any smell of liquor, fighting each other when Kate had visited Barney. And the "middle-ear trouble" chronicled doubtfully by a neighbor.

Kate lifted her eyes, because this was a thing that had to be certain. "How do you know?"

"I'm a summer bird here myself," said Carpenter, giving her an odd glance, "but my aunt's lived in this town most of her life. She has channels, and she managed to find out about the state business yesterday. She also wangled the Maynards' Bridgeport telephone number out of some board or other—they must have told some story about giving the boy a vacation with friends, as I can't believe they'd be allowed to move about like that; there are regular check-up visits—and," Carpenter said with a look of satisfaction, "I telephoned last night and gave Maynard a very large scare. I would bet that Barney is now up to his knees in ice cream."

"But he can't stay with them," said Kate instantly.

"No. But if a few days went by, while the dust settled ... Of course, that's up to you."

Kate studied the bottom of her glass. For the first time since she had felt the cruel pressure on the back of her head, she allowed her mind to dwell directly on what, at the end, Georgia had tried to do. How patient she had been until then—steel under the cream, hatred under the soft caressing laugh—and how correspondingly furious when all her work was undone, because Robert's widow was to escape her after all. She had probably not seen Kate at the wheel of the car, but the woman who had destroyed Robert ...

Kate did not know that she shivered. The last little wisp of ice in her glass melted, and she realized that she felt nothing about Georgia at all except a sense of deliverance. If you were healed of a dreadful wound, you did not want to keep the bandage. Georgia could be a Barlow to the last, heedless of her own safety as she ran to get help for her injured daughter-in-law.

Carpenter was watching her quietly. Kate, the last vestiges of remoteness gone, saw that he looked very tired. Both he and his aunt had been up all night, over the horrifying death of someone they both knew well, while she had slept so obliviously at the hospital. She smiled at him unconsciously, and his face changed; without a word he took her glass and his own and vanished into the kitchen.

It might have been the rain, or the drink, or the feeling of complete safety; Kate said almost dreamily when Carpenter came back, "I thought yesterday that you'd gone to New York."

"I told Georgia I was going. I thought . . ."

He said in a new brisk practical voice that he had been concerned about Kate for weeks, and that he had begun to wonder what satisfaction could be gotten out of the mailed newspaper clippings except by someone who was there to see her reaction. "Then, when I saw one of those wasp reports in the newspaper I wondered if I could pin it down. The night you came to the cottage I went to the house—"

He had proved nothing, he said; in answer to his idle request for the newspaper, in order to show an editorial to Gerald, there had been vague glances around but the newspaper was not forthcoming. But he had carried away a strong impression that someone was very pleased at his expressed worry over Kate; it meant that her condition was marked and noticeable.

"It seemed incredible that if I was right you wouldn't have even a suspicion," said Carpenter dryly, "but when I tried to find out who you thought was sending the clippings, and why, you implied very strongly that I turned your stomach."

Kate blushed vividly. "You could have told me."

"With not a scrap of proof? Would you have believed me?"

Kate took refuge in lighting a cigarette. Carpenter went on to say that when he had telephoned late the afternoon before, and been told by Joanna that Kate wasn't there and hadn't been there all day, he could only conclude that she was gone on some errand connected with the Maynards.

"I didn't like the sound of it. So I called Georgia and said good-bye and borrowed a friend's car—I had a hunch that if anything was going to happen to you it wouldn't happen on the premises. I sat for several years in the driveway of a vacant house near the corner," said Carpenter concisely, "and then you drove by. Maybe to get cigarettes or something to read—but about twenty minutes later Joanna's car came out. I couldn't tell who was driving, but I followed. I nearly lost you both at a light," his face was grim at the memory, "and then I picked you up at the motel. It began to look as though you were being run off the road—and then you turned off."

With the darkness in the car humming and stirring about her. Kate glanced instinctively at the still-visible sting on her wrist.

Carpenter said, "Georgia must have been quick, at the motel. I found a broken wasp's nest not far from your car last night. I'd guess that she put it under the hood, and when the engine warmed up . . ."

"But I drove," said Kate wonderingly; it was like looking at a set of X rays and finding that you were fine after all.

"Yes. You're free," said Carpenter, with an echo of last night's emptiness. "You don't need shoring-up any more."

Kate met his eyes and his regretful half-smile steadily. She thought of how bereft she had felt when Georgia had conveyed his good-byes, and she thought about Barney, who was going to need at least interim care. She thought ridiculously that if she dropped a plate or bumped into a lamp, Carpenter would think it the most natural thing in the world.

"Everybody needs shoring-up," she said.

156

She did not see Joanna again, except at the funeral; she learned much later that Joanna had said with the Barlow coolness and strength, "I don't hold Kate responsible, but I would really rather not see her."

Madge Perlmutter Ingham said to a friend at her wedding reception, "It's too bad the Barlows couldn't be here. There's Joanna, of course, and Robert's widow—I understand she's marrying again, and there's talk of some small boy. *Really*. When you think that Georgia died trying to save her . . . but she was a wonderfully devoted woman. There was nothing she wouldn't have done for Robert's wife."